Granny's No Angel

by

Ciara Threadgoode

~Past Life~

A woman of quality
Poised and graced
The rage within
The calm of her face
The warmth of her eyes, the lash of her tongue
The warmth of her body, like that of the sun
A woman of dignity
The fairy with wings
The blood line of queens
A mistress of kings
Intuitive and powerful
Second to none, she wears the scars of battles won
Her soul is a light that shines through her eyes
She bears in the open without a disguise
Judge not this woman, for she is no fool
At the hand of no man, her life she will rule
Now I tell you this and it's not in jest
She's slipped through your fingers
You've just lost the best.

Donna Bishop

Table of Contents

Chapter One

Spanks Left Me Saddened

Chapter Two

Episodes

Chapter Three

Looking Forward

Chapter Four

This Changes Everything

Chapter Five

 On Top of a Pickle

Chapter Six

New Digs

Chapter Seven

We Definitely Kissed

Chapter Eight

The Fudge Factor

Chapter Nine

Guardian Angels

Chapter Ten

A Tale Of Two Mothers

Chapter Eleven

Granny's Famous Potato Salad

Chapter Twelve

Good News And A Bad Odor"

Chapter Thirteen

A Surprise Visit

Chapter Fourteen

She Was Right

Chapter Fifteen

The Reality Sets In

Chapter Sixteen

What Now

Chapter Seventeen

The Showdown

Chapter Eighteen

Candle Light, Candle Bright

Chapter Nineteen

Only A Dream

Chapter Twenty

Saying It Out Loud

Chapter Twenty-One

Taking The First Step

Chapter Twenty-Two

Out With The Old, And The New Is Really Good

Chapter Twenty-Three

Transformations

Chapter Twenty-Four

The Sun Will Come Out Tomorrow

Chapter One
Spanks Left Me Saddened

August 16, 2013

The house was dark and I could see the candle flickering wildly as I moved down the staircase. The same dance it did most times I lit it, only this time, like others, the candle had lit itself; my sign that she is here. It was happening several times a month now. At first it had been more frequent. She'd slowed down a tad and I'd be lying if I said that it hadn't worried me. Gene didn't believe me at first, because he couldn't hear her. I was the only one able to hear her voice and grasp the reality of her messages. The dogs sensed her presence too. It has been more than a year since Granny passed away but it hasn't seemed that long to me because a little more than a month after Gene and I had laid her body to rest in her hometown of Truckee California, she began showing up in the middle of the night. I couldn't see her at first, but I could hear her voice as clearly as if she were sitting down next to me. This night would be our last meeting.

The first time she appeared, I was having trouble sleeping. We had been cleaning her house, preparing things to be sold at an estate sale, per her written request. I'd tossed and turned until finally, I climbed out of bed, going downstairs to have some wine, leaving Gene and the dogs sleeping. I'd lit a candle and was sitting at the kitchen table when it happened. Without warning, the flame was almost extinguished, and then exploded as if some type of accelerant had been thrown on it. It felt almost like a scene from one of those spooky ghost movies I'd watched with Gene. I'd consumed two glasses of wine before it happened, so I just sat and watched the entire spectacle with my mouth open. When the flame resumed its normal illumination, I felt a warm squeeze, almost like a hug, before I heard her voice. My emotional radar was confused. I felt comforted yet vaguely apprehensive too.

"Cherry dear," the voice said. I picked up the cork and quickly placed it in the bottle, then turned to put it back in the refrigerator when the voice spoke again.

"Cherry, don't be alarmed. It's me, child." I felt my body begin to shake as if I were standing in a walk-in freezer and then a warm rush of love ran through me. I sat back down, reopening the

Granny's No Angel 2

bottle and poured the remaining wine into my glass. *Holy hell I thought, I might need a program and maybe a sponsor too.*

"No dear, you're okay," the voice said.

I barely remember asking, "Granny, are you okay?" and her response was lightning quick, maybe to keep me from thinking the obvious; I was losing it.

"Yes dear, I'm just fine." I took a quick sip from my glass.

"Why can't I see you?" I asked. Several moments passed before she responded.

"I'm not completely sure. I might not be doing it correctly," she replied. "I was only given a few minutes of instruction and you know me, dear. I'm slow out of the gate and I've always marched to my own drummer." I thought I heard a hint of a snicker in her voice. It helped.

My fear subsided and my curiosity heightened. "Are you stuck here or did you not want to leave?" I asked the candle flame.

"Oh dear, I was more than ready to leave. I just wasn't finished. It's much different here than I ever imagined," she confessed.

I took another sip from my glass, pondering her words, when from the corner of my eye, I saw something move on the staircase. When I turned and looked more closely, I saw five little red doxies, sitting completely still, watching the candle as if they were in a deep trance. I turned back to the flame.

"Yes, dear," the voice said, before I had a chance to ask, "Spanks is here with me." Spanky, a stocky red short-haired Dachshund had been the only guy in my life before my husband Gene and I met. He'd suddenly and unexpectedly taken leave of his physicality here while in Granny's care not long before her own passing.

I felt my lips turn up into a slight smile and a tear brimmed in my right eye. This was only the beginning of many strange things to come. In the book The Second Diary Granny had been recording her personal perspectives on her family's quirks, most guarded secrets, her own childhood memories of rural life and her daily experiences that included a joyful romantic romp during the months preceding her passing. Following are the final three days of handwritten entries from her secret diary.

Day Sixty-One

Well the kids let me plumb off the hook as I knew they would. Those two coddle this old woman something fierce. While I still feel that I should have been able to do something more for little Spanks, they said that he was ready to go; it was his time, and things happened just as they should have. I wish now that I would have thought to do CPR or something. I just froze when it happened and my seventy-six years of wisdom wasn't worth a lick of spit. I'll never forgive myself for that.

Gene and Cherry took his tiny canine body to their vet to be cremated and left me with the other babies while they were gone. I could barely look any of them in the eye. Jennifer jumped up on the sofa when I settled in and laid her head on my lap. It was comforting until I looked over at that empty dog bed and felt my heart drop to my stomach. My water works immediately sprang a leak and I must have cried me a river for a full thirty minutes.

I'm not completely sure if it was because of Spanks or not, but for the first time while the kids were out, I noticed when I sat completely still, I could feel my heart clunking away in my chest like a stalled locomotive and it throbbed really hard for three or four beats, almost skipping a beat or two. At first, it scared the bejeezus out of me. Then there was an unfamiliar queasiness and my body grew hotter than a nanny goat in a pepper patch. I fetched a cold washcloth for my face and after a spell I was right as rain again. Maybe my heart really did break some when that little guy crossed the rainbow bridge. I know his death hit me harder than times I'd lost some of the humans in my life. Before the kids returned, I got a call from Heather. She hadn't heard about Spanks and I didn't tell her. She wanted to chat, and some grandmotherly advise I think, but unfortunately, I just wasn't in the right mind for it. I did as much listening as I could before telling her I wasn't feeling up to par and that I'd call her back tomorrow.

I decided maybe it was time to put something in my belly. I'd waited until morning to call the kids about Spanks; there was no real reason to wake them from a sound sleep only to give them awful news, so I'd only had one cup of coffee before they arrived and had forgotten to take my pills. I poured myself cup number two and washed down my pills before rummaging through the fridge. I found a slice of peach pie for me and a package of kosher hotdogs for the doxies. With very little coaxing, they joined me and we had us a little memorial service of our own. I'm not sure if Cherry had plans for that package of hot dogs, but we thoroughly enjoyed them. She didn't seem upset with me when she returned home from the vet's office. I didn't mention the little episode with my old ticker and unless it happens again, I'm just going to chalk it up to grief and sadness; why make a mountain out of a mole hill? The kids sure don't need me acting like a needy nincompoop right now. None of the dogs stayed with me tonight, so I think I'll go make me a cup of tea and watch some TV to get my mind off everything, and hopefully calm this dull, achy feeling in my stomach.

Treasured Friend

I lost a treasured friend today
The little dog who used to lay
Her gentle head upon my knee
And shared her silent thoughts with me....

She'll come no longer to my call
Retrieve no more her favorite ball
A voice far greater than my own
Has called her to His golden throne.

Although my eyes are filled with tears
I thank Him for the happy years
He let her spend down here with me
And for her love and loyalty.

When it is time for me to go
And join her there, this much I know....
I shall not fear the transient dark
For she will greet me with a bark.

~Author Unknown~

Chapter Two
Episodes

Day Sixty-Two

Well, dadgum if it didn't happen again today. I'm not sure what in the Sam Hill is going on with me, but I'm thinking that maybe this old gal is finally reaching her expiration date. This time when my episode happened, I was standing in the kitchen pouring myself a cup of coffee. It was all I could do to grab hold of the counter to keep myself from landing in a pile on the floor. When I collected myself, I was of a good mind to tell Cherry what I was experiencing as soon as she arrived. After I settled on the sofa, feeling good as gold again, though, I changed my mind. I could see in my mind's eye the awful domino effect that telling her would set off. She'd get worried and then cart me off to the emergency room, and once there, some doctor would admit me, and when all was said and done, I'd end up just like Raylan did. I believe if something is going to happen, I'd just like to be here in my own home, all comfy as a marshmallow in bed. All day my mind bounced around, thinking of what I wanted to say to all my kinfolk, just in case my suspicions proved true. I could tell that Cherry suspected something was up with me as soon as she came in the door, and though it was tough, I kept my mouth closed tighter than a lid on a coffin. The girl didn't deserve to be forced on one more emotional roller coaster ride.

The kids hadn't been here an hour when Gene announced that he and Cherry had an errand to run and asked me if I minded watching the rug rats. Of course I didn't mind, but they both kept staring at me all skeptical-like. It felt as if I had a red dot on my forehead, marked for a sniper's bullet. Almost as if they somehow already knew about my episodes without me ever saying a word. Again, I was just about ready to fess up and admit what was going on with me when Ryan, bless his little heart, waltzed over to my walker and hiked up his leg.

Gene shouted, "Holy crap on a cracker," which was almost as funny to me as what the little doxie had done. He reached down and swooped up the pooch, rocketing to the back door like a guided missile.

Rivers of embarrassment washed over poor Cherry's face; then we both locked eyeballs and burst out laughing like loonies in *a lockdown. That worrisome, awkward moment had passed and I felt a satisfying sense of achievement, like when that last piece of a five-thousand-piece puzzle is popped into place.*

After the kids left, I gave Heather a call back and what I thought would be a ten-minute call turned into an hour-long therapy session. Gene would've called it a pity party, and I'd have agreed with his call.

Funny how that boy's ways are rubbing off on me. Several times during the one-sided conversation, I had to keep reminding myself, I was born with two ears and one mouth for a reason, and then there was the occasional, "Dot, shut your pie hole" about a half dozen times, too. It seems that her husband, Jackson, who seems to think the sun comes up just to hear him crow, won't change companies or find a different type of employment, even though the outfit he works for is shadier than a vegetarian eating tacos at a Jack-in-the-Box. The employees often don't get paid in a timely fashion and with four young mouths to feed it's been quite worrisome for my granddaughter. He's convinced her that he's doing the best he can, but I do believe she's at the end of her rope, has tied a knot in the end and is hanging on for dear life.

Before meeting Jackson, Heather was a freelance artist, selling her paintings and such at various art shows and galleries around town and doing quite well for herself. Once they married and had their first child, she quit painting altogether to stay home and raise her children. Jackson was a car salesman; she'd met him when she purchased her first car at the dealership where he was employed. They'd only dated a short while, three months if my memory serves me right, and I've often wondered if that wasn't a decision she now regrets. I know she loves that litter of hers, but she's home with them twenty-four-seven and I believe she's feeling like raisin' kids with so few and uncertain resources is equivalent to being pecked to death by a crazed chicken. Heather was always the closest to her mother; her siblings just weren't as clingy as she was and I believe Peg realized that about her and rather enjoyed it. Things began to fold between Heather and her mom, like a wet deck of cards, a year or so after Jackson came into the picture. I believe Peggy realized she was no longer the center of her daughter's attention and was losing her manipulative powers to a much more cunning manipulator. Heather had traded up, so to speak and gotten herself some sex and children in the deal.

Granny's No Angel 12

Heather and Peg didn't speak much for a good year or so until my daughter finally accepted that Jackson might just be in a better position to control things; especially since mother and daughter rarely saw each other, so she changed her strategy and went on the defense. Heather and Peg eventually patched things up but I always felt that, that child just became the net on a ping pong table, smack dab between two crazed control freaks, fighting each other through her. Just as I realized Heather's end of the phone had become quiet, Ryan let out a strange cough; the other dogs and I gave him a long look. Then, out of nowhere, she asked if I'd mind if she and the kids came to stay the weekend with me, for two whole days. For a moment I thought she was joking, but then I realized something appalling. She was serious.

I quickly told her in my sweetest voice, "Honey, I love you so much but I'm just not in any shape to entertain a house full of children."

After a pause that was way too long, Heather said, "Maybe I'll ask Cherry and Gene."

I didn't chuckle, but I sure could have because I knew that that idea would go over with them like a tough turd in a punch bowl. Cherry loves her sister and her young ones, but she and her husband are quite content with their childless life. I know better than anyone because I've tried my hardest to push them over to the dark side, *as Gene so cleverly calls it.*

They did tell me yesterday that they planned on checking with some dachshund rescues here in Santa Barbara to help fill the gap they both felt in their hearts after losing Spanks. The bonus I see there is that the critter will come with a normal doggy-type name, maybe. Getting Gene to be okay with normal is like trying to put underwear on an alligator though.

Heather went on to tell me that her brother Michael had a new girlfriend she didn't much care for. She said he'd met her at a bar a couple weeks ago and had recently tried sneaking the poor gal into Peg's house at three in the morning. Of course they got caught, Michael's always been a few grains short of a full silo and Peg hit the roof, telling him he was no longer allowed to bring his kids there for his weekend visits.

Heather said he then showed up at her house with the same woman, asking if they could stay with her for a spell. She was appalled that he'd bring some barfly to stay with her family, someone she said would have to sneak up to a water fountain to get a drink. It's my guess that Michael Scott was desperate; the girl had a pulse after all. The boy hasn't been known for thinking with his brain. His biggest priority in life is having fun and then to add fuel to his difficulties, he learned that Dustin is his biological father. Who knows what's really bouncing around in that boy's noggin at this point? I guess I'll give him a call, too. As soon as Heather took a breath, and with one of her youngins yelling in the background, "milk, milk, lemonade, round the corner fudge is made" at the top of his lungs, I told her I needed to go to the powder room; which wasn't a fib. Our conversation ended with, always try to remember, you must break a few eggs in life to make yourself a proper omelet. She said okay, but I'm not sure if the girl grasped what it was I was really saying to her. I was hoping that she'd interpret my words to mean, rather than keeping all her eggs in one basket, or doing what's obviously not working, she might have to crack her normal routine and stir things up a bit, so she and those kids of hers can have a better life. Although everyone wants to keep their families intact, sometimes just one rotten egg makes all the others sick. Maybe Cherry would be better at explaining it to her sister.

When the kids returned, they got busier than bees in a cornfield . Cherry started making us some lunch and Gene began tidying up the place, flashing all of us a grin every few minutes, displaying his perfect white teeth. I just sat perched on the sofa, with five little doxies, watching all the action. These days, most folks don't relax as enthusiastically as the dogs and I do. It's a darned shame, too. Well I believe it's tea time. Since no one's here to stop us, I think Miss Lopez and I might have a few cookies.

Chapter Three
Looking Forward

Day Sixty-Three

Well I've gotten a lot accomplished today and when I finish up here and finally head off to bed, I'll have no regrets or remorse. I spoke to Michael Scott today and I believe he and I did some significant soul searching about the path he's been on and the road he wants to take now. Life is rarely just black and white, and today's kids seem to be growing up in a society that is extremely self-indulgent. I tried to explain that we each get to choose our own life colors, and as parents we teach by example, always doing our best to be decent, loving, caring human beings. We're not always going to say and do the right things, and that's fine. It's our intention that counts.

I reminded him that life is full of opportunities, dressed up as challenges and sometimes you need to wear a helmet; maybe even goggles and you can always, always laugh at yourself.

I believe in my heart the child will be okay. I'd had my mind made up to call each of my children today, but after I'd rolled it around some last night, over not one, but two cups of tea, I decided against it. I realize that the world has changed and children have changed with it. I am one grateful old woman to have all the beautiful memories of each of my children when they were sweet, loving, and much too busy growing up to be engaged in mean and hateful behavior. That thought made my decision not to call any of them a lot easier for me to live with. Yes, way too often, my expectations and their behavior were not the best match, but I'm comforted somewhat, in knowing that where they stood then and where they stand now are not places for me to judge. People do what they do, even your closest kin. My dear mother used to say "No sense looking at sour grapes. Show me the sweet things in life." When my kids were young, I put them all up on their own separate pedestals. If by doing that, I wronged you, please forgive me. I speak from my heart when I say I did my very best. When I look in the mirror, I am just fine with the person looking back at me. I've managed over the last month or so to write each of them a personal letter and that script is being held by my lawyer who will distribute each document when the time comes.

The first time it seemed real, and I seriously contemplated the reality that I might actually be leaving all of you was early last night after the kids went home. I thought about many things during the evening, so many things that I needed an extra cup of tea. Tonight, I have a kind of inner acknowledgment that I'm edging closer to my journey to other places. I'm on my way to finding out what's really going to happen, if anything, in the next chapter of my life and I'm happy to say that it's as exciting as the best magical story I ever could have read. I'm sad to have to leave many of you; especially my granddoggies, but I'm hopeful I'll see you all again.

When I was growing up, we had an old hound dog named Chester, a pot-licker my pop used to call him. I loved that dog with everything I had and then some. He was always happy-go-lucky and as hungry as a mosquito in a nudist camp. He lived to be twelve and I reckon I look forward to scratching that old boy behind the ears again. And of course, I want to see dear little Spanks. I'm hoping, as some have assured me, that my legs will be as they once were and I'll be able to take both dogs for a romp in nature; maybe even go to the ocean and wiggle my toes in the soft cool sand. I'd like that even more than a sassy cat would love a good scrap. And I do so look forward to seeing my folks. My biggest blessing and gift in life has been the upbringing my parents gave me. It was simple and honest. We didn't always have the biggest or best of everything, but what we had, we appreciated. Having each other's love and respect was worth more than any old electrical gadget. It seems like folks these days just don't think about each other like we did back then. I can't wait to hear my mother's sweet voice again. I miss the talks she and I had when I was a little girl; while she sat behind me and brushed my long brown hair. I'm a tad worried about seeing both Bert and Raylan together. Bert's going to act like someone just licked the red right off his candy cane, I'm sure. Poor Raylan. And I already have a to-do list as long as my arm, all made up in my mind. All the things I'll be able to do with ease and without pain or a darned walker. Nora and I are going to go dancing, and make a crazy quilt, and read all the books in the world I wasn't able to read in this lifetime. I'm going to lose the dress, put on some cozy sweatpants, and eat cake. Heck, I'm going to eat anything I want and drink lots and lots of tea. Yes, I'm ready for my next big adventure.

Granny's No Angel 20

Chapter Four
This Changes Everything

June 2nd, 2013 marked one year since my grandmother's passing. So much had happened in that year. On Monday July 2nd, one month to the day of her departure, each family member received a type written, letter from her lawyer, stating her wishes regarding distribution of her personal belongings. Unbeknownst to everyone but Gene and me, she'd amended her original will and completely overhauled it. After reading our copy of the letter, I'd secretly wished I could've been a fly on my mother's wall when she opened hers. She'd been so sure that she'd had things tightly sewn up when it came to handling her mother's affairs. I could almost envision the look on her face. Who *doesn't* want to see a volcano erupt with all those red hot cinders, and hot lava? I knew that everyone in the family was caught off guard, just as Gene and I were.

A few days after Granny's funeral service in Santa Barbara, but before we made the trip to Truckee with her body, I received a phone call from Nolan Gretsky, Granny's lawyer. He'd had all the locks changed on the house, per her written instruction. we were to come by and pick up the new keys, along with a list of items to be distributed to individual family members. Each one was to receive one personal item, and all of her other belongings were to be sold at an estate sale. She was adamant and crystal clear about her wishes. Mr. Gretsky told me that I'd be informed later how the proceeds from the sale would be dispersed. Before I allowed him to end our call, I convinced him that unless he wanted to see news of my demise flashed over the local TV station that evening, he was going to have to make one additional call after we hung up. That call would be to Melanie Margarita Legg. I wanted her to hear firsthand that Gene and I had nothing to do with the changing of the locks. Reluctantly, he agreed to make the call. He must have heard stories about Peg firsthand from my grandmother. I was just relieved to know that I'd live to see another day.

Of course I'd already known that Brock Henry, my Uncle Brock, was to get the colorful quilt that Granny had so lovingly hand sewn. My grandmother had told me herself she wanted him to have it and made me promise to see to it the day we took it from the dusty box Dustin had fetched from the attic for her.

Reese Rose, my Aunt Cricket, was to receive a beautiful oak-inlaid jewelry box my grandfather Bert had made. Penelope Candice, PC, was to have my grandfathers extensive gun collection that had been stored in a closet floor safe that neither Gene nor I even knew existed. My grandmother had given Mr. Gretsky the combination, to allow us access. Erin Jacqueline, Peanut, was to have Granny's collection of novels, and believe me when I say it was a library of books. Melanie Margarita, my mother Peg, was to get the four -poster bed her Pop had made for my grandparents as a wedding present. That gift and the reasoning behind it was the only one that didn't make any sense to me. My mother had a bed; in fact, since all her children were grown and had left home, she'd bought several sets of bedroom furniture to fill the empty rooms. Why would my grandmother want her to have an old piece of furniture that obviously wouldn't match anything else she owned? This question baffled Gene and me for the longest time.

Each of the grandchildren received a personal handwritten letter. Heather, Michael, me, and PC's only daughter Savanna, were the recipients. But there were a whole slew of great grandchildren. Each of them was gifted with savings bonds that were safely tucked away in a bank safety deposit box, the key to be in Mr. Gretsky's possession until the children were adults. This arrangement totally upset Jackson, who decided to tell the lawyer, Gene, and me in great detail just how much it upset him. I felt really sorry for Mr. Gretsky. Gene and I were used to the *I-am-the-children's-parent* speeches he often dished out when he wasn't given access to the kids' money, but Nolan Gretsky was only fulfilling my grandmother's wishes.

My mother had taken all her grandchildren to the bank to start their own savings accounts years ago. If she gave them money for a birthday or other holidays she took them to the bank to deposit half of the amount they were given. They were then taken on a shopping trip to purchase whatever they wanted with the remaining money. This strategy began when Peg caught wind that Jackson was requiring each family member to contribute any money they received, gift or otherwise, to the *family pot*. Yes, my eyes are rolling here. Jackson suffers from delusions of grandeur and although I'm a hundred percent sure he doesn't think so, everyone who knows him and his philosophies would agree with my evaluation. This dude is a narcissist, and to add to that other scary psychological diagnoses I couldn't begin to define.

It was just days before the last presidential election when Jackson had asked Gene and me who we were going to vote for, while we were over visiting the kids. That was the last day we spoke to him. Gene, reluctantly divulged the candidate he'd chosen and Jackson blatantly laughed in his face, "Don't give up your daydream." he spat. It was obvious that anyone not voting for the same candidate as Jackson Miller, was just plain stupid. Either my sister didn't hear the conversation or didn't feel his demeanor was inappropriate, I'm not really sure. Gene and I decided then that if my sister was happy, we'd just distance ourselves from him, his holier-than-thou negative behavior and wish them both the best. When it's family, what else can you do?

July 5th was the first evening my grandmother showed up, at least her voice did, at our kitchen table. On July 14th, Gene and I returned to the Santa Barbara Animal Rescue, where we'd submitted our application to adopt a new family member. We both wanted so many of them; it was impossible to look into those sweetly animated little faces that were clearly saying, "Just stop and look into my eyes, you love me already, you know you do," and not want them all, but we felt that we had to settle on one. It was the best decision for our family. I had to be strong. Gene had come into the building strong, but now he was waffling. He was like a runner on third base with the ball coming straight at him. He was the weak link. I totally was the stronger of the two of us, but then, I admit it, I caved. We adopted two females. A seven-year-old black and tan short-haired Dachshund named *Pretzel* (ours were all red) and a ten-year-old black and tan long-haired Chihuahua, *Taco* that Gene absolutely would not go home without. He was threatening a full-fledged tantrum, and no one wanted to see that. I really did everyone at the shelter a favor. They turned out to be a perfect fit for our clan.

During our car ride home with the girls, I reminded my tender-hearted husband that now, this very minute, Brad, Ryan, and he were totally outnumbered, gender-wise. He just smiled into our little Chihuahuas face and assured me *the boys* would be sure to treat *the girls* to a parade later, after he changed their *names*.

Chapter Five
On Top of a Pickle

Sunday, July 15, 2012

It was late; maybe eleven-forty-five or so when I awoke. I hadn't really looked at the clock, but that's what it felt like. Gene and I had tucked the dogs in and had gone to bed early. We'd finally finished up at Granny's house and everything was ready for the estate sale. We were tired, *dog* tired. Tomorrow, as Gene had re-named Miss Taco, was in a playpen next to the foot of the bed and gave me a pitiful bark as I passed on my way to the door. We were told by the staff that her previous owner, an elderly woman who'd passed away, had no family to leave her with. The woman had been confined to a wheelchair the last two years and wasn't able to take her out regularly, so the little girl had taken up squatting whenever and wherever she could. A habit we would surely work on. For now, she had a soft, fluffy bed and a pee pad in her playpen, and Brad. He was the designated cuddler for our little newcomer and had curled his long, ten-pound body around all eight pounds of her. It was an adorable sight to see. And they'd grown quite fond of each other, which was perfect.

Our California King bed was full of the rest of the clan. Pretzel was still Pretzel. Gene hadn't figured out her perfect name yet; it had only been one day into her adoption, and honestly, I was pretty sure it wasn't at the top of her "worry" list. She was just happy to be in a warm bed surrounded by wieners that all looked like her.

As I tip-toed down the staircase, I noticed the candle on the kitchen table wasn't lit, and I felt disappointed. Three nights ago I'd come down at a much later hour, to find the candle glowing brightly and a feeling of my grandmother's presence; almost boastful that she'd been clever enough to figured out a way to do it. We'd only had a short chat before she announced that she had to go, which was way sooner than I'd have liked. She'd surprised me with her visit last time, and I'd been tongue-tied, but this time I had questions, and I was hoping for some solid answers. As I stood in front of the open refrigerator assessing my snack choices, I grabbed a package of Swiss cheese, thinking that it would complement my glass of white wine. Just as the door clicked shut,

I turned to see the candle wick become a glowing flame. The cheese slid from my hand and hit the floor but I managed to hold onto the wine bottle. Granny was in the house. I sat down at the kitchen table and poured myself a glass of Pinot Grigio and waited.

If someone had asked me two months before my grandmother passed if it were possible to speak to the dead, I'd have blatantly laughed in their face. That evening, at the kitchen table, the laugh lines had softened. Granny told me once that a closed mouth gathers no foot. And that granny-ism was making perfect sense to me at that moment. When I'd heard stories of people talking to dead relatives or loved ones on talk shows, I just told myself that people see what they want to see, or they just have really overactive imaginations. And as I sat there , talking to a candle flame I realized, that I could have been a little more open minded. At that very moment, my confident, tough-as-nails, and a-whole-lot-of-cynical persona was thinking that maybe there are things in this world that cannot be explained.

Gene didn't believe me. He'd pretty much decided that I was still depressed and that I was hearing my grandmother's voice as a way to help me with closure and accepting the loss.

Or, that I was in a hellacious, drunken stupor. After his initial reaction to my sharing the details of Granny's first visit, he wore a look on his face that said the cheese had completely slipped off my cracker. So I said nothing more. Maybe I was the only one able to pick up what she was putting down. All I knew for sure was that I didn't want her visits to end. Not yet. I didn't fully understand why I was hearing her, but I wasn't ready for it to stop. I'd decided I wanted her company more than I wanted to question my sanity.

"Cherise, how are you, baby girl?" I smiled, snapping myself out of the lull of my thoughts and tried to picture her sweet smiling face, rosy cheeks and all.

"Granny, I'm happier than a tick on a fat dog right now." She laughed her silly laugh and it was like music to my ears. "I have so many questions for you. Why can't you just stay here all the time with Gene and me? He thinks I've gone totally bonkers but if you'd stay and he heard your voice, he'd be on board with everything. It could be just like it was...before." I reached for my glass and took a long sip, without even tasting it, as I mentally re-played that last sentence. *Really, Cherry, that was just stupid. It could never be like it was before. Your grandmother is buried in a grave next to her parents in Truckee, and you're sitting here in the middle of the night drinking wine and talking to a candle flame. That really seems pathetic.*

"It's not at all pathetic, Cherise, and although my tired, worn-out body is indeed buried in Truckee, I am truly here."

I believe my mouth must have fallen open. *How'd she do that? How'd she know what I was thinking?* Panic coursed through me. I needed to focus on the fact that she *was* truly here. Period.

"Cherise, they warned us that not every person having a physical experience would be able to cope with a visit from a person in transition, and believe me when I say, you're the only one I thought would be able to handle it. Please don't be afraid.

I won't be able to stay long. I've been given an assignment. A sort of challenge, you might say, that if I can pull off successfully, will allow me to go to the tippy- top of the pyramid; take a vacation of sorts from any more visits to earth.

It's very complicated, and because my guide told me that letting the cat out of the bag is a lot easier than putting it back in, there's really only so much I'm able to tell you."

Without any thought, I just blurted out, "Granny, I don't understand what all that means. Please don't leave," and then my bottom lip began to quiver involuntarily.

"Now child, you suck that right up; no crying, ya hear?" I wiped the tear that had escaped my right eye and nodded my head in a yes motion. "I'm not sure how I can best explain this to you with the constraints they've placed on me. Okay, let's try this. Remember that sandwich shop Gene likes so much next to the Pet Smart?" I nodded my head, reaching for my glass. "Okay, remember how they put a pickle on top of the sandwich with one of those colored toothpicks?" I continued bobbing my head, "Yes, the Lunch Sack. You hated it when they did that because you said it made the bread all soggy." "Yes, Cherise, and it really did, too. Alrighty, imagine you and Gene are on the bottom slice of one of those delicious sandwiches. You're on the bottom piece." I felt my forehead crinkle up, but I didn't make a sound. "I am now, at this very moment, hanging out with the meat and cheese part of that sandwich. If I'm not able to accomplish the assignment, I'll have to move up to the top piece of bread, but if I complete the challenge, I get to sit up top on the juicy green pickle. That's the place to be if you want a break from this whole cotton pickin' reincarnation boloney. Does that make any sense to you, Cherry?"

I thought about it for a moment, zoning out briefly, picturing my grandmother on top of a sandwich, riding a huge pickle, but that was probably the wine. "Yes, I believe so," I answered quickly. "So what is it exactly that you have to do?" A full minute passed. She seemed to be trying to choose her words carefully, like a cautious parent would tell a six-year-old about the birds and the bees.

"Well, there's a woman stuck here. She doesn't want to move up. She didn't want to leave and she's kinda like a piece of bubble gum on the bottom of a shoe right now. And, she's plumb stubborn and a bit of a rascal too. I have to convince her to move up and on. After spending yesterday with her, I believe she's going to be the death of me," and she giggled. I laughed, too. Even dead, or whatever she was, Granny was hilarious. "Well sweet girl, I'm sad to say that it's about time for me to get going, but I'll be

Granny's No Angel 33

back." Panic struck my belly again. "No Granny, I'm not finished yet. Please stay." "Dear, I wish I could, but Miss Charlotte is getting into trouble again and I need to get over there before all hell breaks loose. Oh my, I made another funny."

"Okay, but Gene and I finally finished getting everything ready for the sale today. The auction is next Saturday. Will you tell me what you want us to do with the money?" my eyes were staring hard into the flame, hoping she hadn't already left.

"Cherise, Mr. Gretsky will tell you soon enough. You two did a wonderful job sorting my things, by the way. I watched you for quite some time today. Thank you. I do appreciate it, Cherry" and the room suddenly grew darker as the light from the flame disappeared. As I watched the smoke twirl toward the ceiling, I knew she was gone.

Chapter Six
New Digs

Saturday, July 21, 2012

After Gene and I had gotten everything ready for the sale, Mr. Gretsky arranged for the company to get inside the house and load up all of Granny's household items and transport them to the auction site. Today at noon, the remainder of her belongings would be put up for sale to the highest bidders. Gene and I decided that even though there wasn't anything left that we wanted, we couldn't stomach watching people, complete strangers, haggle over her things, so we decided not to go. It made me nauseous just thinking about it. The previous weekend we'd walked out of her front door with the personal satisfaction that we'd done what she'd asked of us.

We'd accomplished what she'd requested. We'd also picked up a few items that *weren't* on our list, with no one the wiser. We'd justified it at the time, just as my grandmother would have. I'd looked to the left, then to the right. Nope, no one else was there.

After we'd locked the door and loaded the dogs into the van, Gene saw the stack of polka dot towels in the back seat and a slow smirk spread across his face. "She'd be down with that," he assured me. I knew in my heart she would be, so it was never given another thought.

That day we would keep our minds off the sale and concentrate on our pooches. There were ears to be cleaned and toenails to be trimmed. And my brother Michael was coming over to pick up his set of keys to Granny's house. Per her new will, Michael could rent her house for a fixed amount of five hundred dollars a month. That amount would never increase as long as he was on time with the payments. If he was late however, the monthly rent would be bumped up twenty-five dollars. The rent could go up to a thousand dollars, and if it did, he'd be out on his ear. Even though the house was older, it had three bedrooms, a large backyard, and a garage. In the current economy, it was a bargain, no matter how you looked at it. Because of my mother's unfounded promises, Michael was not thrilled with the terms. To say that he was miffed would be a huge understatement. He'd thought the house was going to fall into his lap, free and clear.

Granny's No Angel 36

When it didn't happen that way, he stormed over to our house, fuming, letter in hand, demanding that Gene and I explain. Because we'd spent time with *our* grandmother, we were expected to know all the reasons behind her decisions. It was assumed that just because we were there a great deal, we would somehow know her reasoning for everything. As my grandmother would have so poetically put it, it was a bunch of hogwash.

At exactly twelve o'clock I ran upstairs to retrieve clippers and Q-tips. Michael wasn't expected for several hours, so we decided to dive in, hunker down, and get 'er done. While I was upstairs I could hear loud banging, which could only be made by a soggy tennis ball ricocheting off walls and other objects around the room. I yelled downstairs at my husband as I always did, and as I made my way back down the stairs, I saw Gene pleading with Ryan to give him the ball, but of course the wiener would not relent. That's just the way it was at our house. Gene and I were outnumbered. I went to the refrigerator and tore a piece of hot dog from an open package. A little enticement never hurt. I squatted down, holding the nibble of meat out to Ryan, who immediately dropped the soggy ball and headed my way for his treat. Trickery, pure and simple.

"You know, Spanks would never have fallen for this," and my heart twisted just a bit as I said the words. I truly missed my little man. We managed to get everyone's ears and toenails done except little Miss Tomorrow's. She pulled her paws away or tucked her head in, so the tail-end of our grooming session was our most challenging. While I baby-talked the little girl, I watched Gene's face express gentle determination, until finally the little Chihuahua allowed us to finish her grooming.

She was still a tad timid, living in a new house with a few clowns short of a circus; so it was understandable. She'd come from a quiet, one-story home with one slow-rolling human and now lived in a two-story fun-house with new brothers and sisters wreaking havoc everywhere she turned. It was going to take some time for her to adjust, and we knew she'd get there eventually. She'd already had zero accidents in the house for a good five days straight. Gene just beamed when another day would pass accident-free. She had definitely wiggled her way into his heart. It was three o'clock and Michael hadn't shown up or called. He'd said he'd be by at two-thirty because he needed to pick his kids up by three from a birthday party they were attending. I dug in my purse for my phone and headed out back to call him. When he picked up, one ring shy of going to voicemail, he was laughing, obviously in the middle of a conversation. I waited for him to excuse himself.

"Yo Cherry," he said as if suddenly remembering he'd told me he'd be over to meet me. "I'm sorry. I totally forgot to call you. My bad." I stood there looking up at the sky, with my phone on speaker and arms crossed tightly over my chest. *Take a deep breath, Cherise, a deep breath.*

"It's almost three-thirty, Michael. Did you already pick the kids up from the party?" I slowly sat down on the cement step and tried to listen to the background noise, but it all sounded like a bunch of yelling and laughing, as if he was outside, at a park maybe? Before I was able to figure it out on my own, Michael spoke up.

"Yeah, about the keys, Sis, I won't need them after all. With my child support payments and all, rent and utilities would just kill me," he announced. Translated, that meant rent and utilities would cut into his party money. My mind was scrambling, trying to figure out his code, or what he was really saying, with absolutely no luck whatsoever.

"So what are you going to do about your weekends with the kids, Mike?" I already knew mom had axed his using her house as a romper room after he'd been busted sneaking some chick in more than a month ago. My sister couldn't dial fast enough to let me know the news. "Oh, I got it covered. It's all cool," he said.

"Okay," and I paused, took a deep breath as my brain scrambled to register what he was *really* saying. "So, some weekend soon, maybe you can bring the kids by so Gene and I can visit with them?" I asked, with maybe a touch too much whine in my voice.

"Yeah sure, or you guys could just come over here and see them," he said a little too quickly. "Where's *here*, Michael?" I asked, with a puzzled expression frozen on my face. "Oh, I'm living with Dustin now," he replied. Oh, Dustin, our *actual* father, I thought.

My stomach suddenly felt as if a young Muhammad Ali had just sucker punched me.

Chapter Seven
We Definitely Kissed

Taking a deep breath, I stood there, just as the back door opened and a herd of weenies almost knocked me back down as they flew by. I looked up at Gene, standing in the door-way, holding Tomorrow protectively, noticing the barest hint of end-of-the-day stubble on his face.

"So?" he prompted, as he bent down and set the Chihuahua on the grass. He followed me into the kitchen.

I sat down, tossing my phone back into my purse. "It seems that my brother is now living with Dustin," I said. Gene stopped in his tracks at the refrigerator and spun back around to face me. "Really?" he said as he reached up to swipe a hand through his perfectly-layered brown locks; his eyes wide with curiosity. "Really," I said. "Even I couldn't make that up," I scoffed. The thing that made this revelation so weird was that Gene and I had attempted to take Michael over to meet Dustin, several weeks after Granny's funeral. They'd seen each other at the church service, but hadn't really spoken. My dad was there and it really was too awkward to try to meet someone, mostly because it was a funeral, so my brother had asked us if we'd take him over for a meet-and-greet, we would be kind of a buffer in case it didn't go well.

Gene and I agreed and I called Dustin and arranged it. He was excited and wanted Mike to meet his girls. As we pulled up in front of the house, my brother and I opened our doors at the curb and waited for Gene to come around. As we stood there, we could see everyone standing at the top of the hill, eagerly waiting for us to join them, when Michael jumped back into our van and shut the door. I looked up to the small crowd and shrugged my shoulders while throwing up my index finger asking them to wait a moment. I crawled back into the passenger's seat and just stared hard at my brother. "We have to go," he stated with a look of panic on his face. "What?" and now Gene was leaning into the van.

"We have to go now," he repeated. That's when he told us. He'd dated one of his new sisters. Gene ran up the driveway and told Dustin that Mike suddenly felt really sick and we were going to take him home. Disappointed, I watched them all wave slowly and start moving toward the house. When Gene got into the driver's side and closed the door, I turned to Michael.

"Please tell me you didn't *do it*?" The look on his face had me worried. I turned toward the windshield and felt my spine tighten. I could feel Gene's eyes on me but my thoughts were pinging in so many directions, I couldn't concentrate on any one of them and I was speechless. This was all sounding like a bad Jerry Springer episode.

Then in a calm quiet voice my brother said, "We definitely kissed, with some tongue, but that's all," and I felt my body loosen up a couple of notches. My hands dropped to my sides and my fingers gripped the edges of the seat under me as if to brace myself for the answer to the question I was about to ask.

"Michael, is there any chance that you were maybe too *drunk* or in an inebriated *haze* to remember whether you two had sex? Please think hard, bro." My words came out breathy, as some unfamiliar fear coursed through my system. Where my brother was concerned, nothing was ever just black or just white. There was always an abundance of fuzzy gray. I let my eyes close as I waited for his answer.

Moments; several long moments that felt like minutes, passed before he finally answered. "Cherise, I'm positive. I remember now that she said she was on her *ladies time*, so nothing happened. I'm sure of it. Actually I never called her back after that. I met another girl and well..."

Gene started the car and we drove in silence to a house where my brother was staying temporarily, his newest flophouse as I chose to call it. Gene and I went home and that was the last contact between Michael and Dustin that we knew about. Apparently, the need for a buffer had passed.

Gene sat down in the chair next to me and we just sat silently for several minutes. "Well, that situation can go either one of two ways," he said finally, "either your brother and Dustin hit it off or it will end up being a full-blown catastrophe," and we stared blankly at each other. I was doubtful that my brother was in it for anything more than a rent-free place to crash, but that was just me, I wasn't always as positive as I could be when it came to Michael. I might also have felt a little jealous. I'd found Dustin and hadn't even had enough one-to-one time with him before my brother just jumped into the middle of it. Gene asked if I wanted to drive over to Dustin's to visit, but I was positive I didn't want to. I really only wanted to talk to Granny at that moment, but of course I didn't tell Gene that. I knew deep down that I was making more of a big deal about my brother and Dustin's relationship than I should be, but it really did sting a little.

If Granny had been there, I'm guessing she'd have said something like, *you only need a little bit of yeast to puff it up to a loaf of bread, it will all be fine.* For just a few seconds, I felt a wisp of her essence seeping into my mind. "Gene? I feel like..." Then something about Michael sort of drifted in. I thought about how much I liked it when I saw him really listening to his kids when they had something to share with him. Suddenly Gene said "You know? I do kind of like the way Michael puts his threads together. I like that he doesn't wear those old-guy dark socks with his shorts and sneaks." We looked at each other with a sort of stunned awareness that there were things we actually admired and appreciated about my brother. It felt good. We felt good.

Chapter Eight

The Fudge Factor

Monday, July 30, 2012, 3:30 a.m.

I sprang straight up, but stayed still while I composed myself to be sure that I didn't wake Gene or the dogs. I'd had this same vivid dream about Heather's son Saxby five times in two weeks now and like all of the other times, the rhythm of my heart felt as if there was a hummingbird trapped inside my chest cavity. My forehead was hot and sweaty and my hands felt clammy. This dream always felt so real.

When no one stirred and the chorus of snoring didn't alter in pitch or tempo, I held my breath and lifted myself up and out of bed. I walked softly on the balls of my feet until I reached the doorway, and then my pace quickened. As I made my way down the stairs, only the night light above the kitchen sink welcomed me.

It had been more than two weeks since my grandmother's last visit and I was concerned. My fear that she was gone for good was beginning to feel like a reality. Rather than cling to the gnawing pain of losing her all over again, I clung to the words that she'd spoken to me on the last Sunday evening we'd visited. *"I'll be back."* she'd assured me.

Right now I just really wanted to hear her voice. The dream was occurring more frequently, and I needed to talk about them. Maybe she'd understand why I was having them. The dream didn't make any sense to me and I knew Gene would just chalk it up to my grief, as he'd done when I mentioned Granny's first visit.

I hadn't been able to share this with anyone and my head was beginning to feel like a bomb ready to explode. I grabbed a bottle of wine from the fridge and some chips from the cabinet and sat down at the table. I lit the candle that was now a permanent fixture. Gene referred to it as our new centerpiece.

After a glass of wine, I began pouring my heart out to the orange flame; a picture I'd never allow any living being witness. Even I felt pathetic, and it was me doing the babbling. But nothing could have prepared me for what came next.

At first I thought I was hallucinating as I focused on what appeared to be a thin line of smoke almost seeming to come from a circular hole in the ceiling and projecting all the way to the floor in a solid line. I stood, then took two steps toward it; staring up, squinting at the ceiling curiously. I was thinking it had to be coming from a hole in the guest bedroom floor above. Just as I whispered *that's just odd*, it disappeared and standing in the kitchen doorway was the dark shape of a human form. I quickly took two giant steps back and stood behind my chair. My heartbeat slowed a little; it had begun to race like a crazed tribal drum, and I watched as the hazy shape began to fill in like a coloring-book picture in slow motion. I felt my breath slowly gravitate toward hyperventilation, waiting, as my eyes zeroed in on the scene in front of me. It was all happening a good thirty feet away.

Breath held tightly, I stared across the room and slowly began to recognize the elderly woman. We both stood perfectly still; well, I did until my eyes took in the image of Granny standing in my kitchen doorway, wearing nothing but a grin. She was naked, closely resembling a human Shar Pei with a gray bun on the back of her head. Startled, I quickly threw my hands over my eyes, but let's face it, you can't un-see something like that. Feeling as if that wasn't enough, I quickly turned around. With my back to her and our only light source behind me, I slowly dropped my hands. For several moments I stared silently at the wall hoping desperately for my grandmother to be dressed so I could turn around and see her. Finally, I couldn't wait another second; I needed to hear her voice. I needed to validate what I'd just seen.

"Granny, are you decent?" I asked, in just above a whisper. My hands were in tight fists, hanging at my sides.

"Gimme a minute, dear," she responded quickly.

Slowly I let out the breath I hadn't realized I was holding in and a giant sense of relief flooded through my body. She *was* here. She was really here with me.

"Okay Cherise, I have a towel around me now. You can turn around," she announced. Apprehension, curiosity and confusion were not enough to stop or slow me down, and I turned around. Yep, there stood my grandmother in a hot-pink towel.

"Sit down, dear. I haven't got much time this trip, and you have many questions for me." I did as I was told and watched as she walked toward the table, stopping several feet from me.

In a voice that I hoped didn't quiver or sound too whiny, I said, "Granny, I was so afraid you weren't coming back. It's been so long," and I watched as an exultant yet triumphant grin spread across her face. I couldn't help but smile back.

"I missed you, too, baby girl. I can't believe I actually pulled this off" and her chest seemed to puff up and out just a bit. "I've had my hands plumb full with Miss Charlotte, and well, she's a real pistol. She doesn't want to leave Las Vegas; we've been hot tub-hopping and she's strangely obsessed with all those Elvis impersonators," she said.

Feeling anxious about her leaving, I just began rattling off questions I wanted her to answer. "Granny, I keep having dreams, well this one dream, over and over again. Each time I have it, a little more detail gets added to it, but it always starts out the same. Saxby's been kidnapped and he's in a cold, dark room, maybe even a basement; only I don't know where the room is. It's like I'm supposed to find him. The dream is terrible and I wake up each time, panicked and worried. I don't understand why I'm having this same dream again and again," I watched her face as I spoke, and she kept nodding her head, as if she already knew about it.

She raised both hands as if to tell me to stop but quickly dropped them when her towel began to fall. After she'd readjusted it, she explained, "I know, dear, and I had every intention of coming sooner so I could explain, and I'm sorrier than a tick on a hairless dog about that. Your dreams are my fault, I'm sorry to say." I took in a deep breath, and my forehead wrinkled, but my eyes were glued firmly to hers, continuing to listen without interrupting.

"It seems that Jackson is going to involve himself in some unsavory shenanigans that cannot end well without *our* help. Just call it one of those guardian angel-type assignments that everyone's always talking about.

When I got here, I was told that before I can leave for that place I was telling you about last time I was here, the next plateau of sorts, I have to tend to Miss Charlotte and take care of this Jackson matter too. And they both have to *end well*. I had no idea that Charlotte was going to be such a wild card, and when I realized how much work she was going to be, I knew I'd have to enlist your help. That's where your dream comes in. It's a way for someone in my predicament to share things with you that we're not allowed to tell you about," and she took her right hand and swished it across her mouth in a zipping motion.

I reached for my glass and took a quick sip. "Sometimes, even though I can't come right out and tell you something because of the rules, I'm allowed to show you in a dream. It's a sort of *angel fudging* that another angel told me about. They figure that people can explain away a dream as just an oddity, caused by a spicy meal or a bad day. For me, it's just like setting up a movie for you to watch when you fall asleep, only I'm new to all of this, and you've been getting re-runs because Miss Charlotte's been swinging from chandeliers and dragging my butt from one casino to another, playing tricks on people. And that's all well and good as long as she sticks to the rules and doesn't cross any lines. But Miss Charlotte's not real concerned about rules or where we go, if you get my drift. She has a new great grandbaby and doesn't want to leave until she's had a chance to put her mitts on him. She doesn't understand being rebellious or not crossing over isn't going to change the fact that she won't be able to hold her granddaughter's son. That's my job, and believe me when I say, I've had more faith in fairy tales than I have in convincing her she needs to move on. I do think she's finally starting to like me though, if only just a smidge."

Granny's No Angel 52

Chapter Nine
Guardian Angels

For a long minute my brain was bombarded with images of Granny and some strange woman in a hot tub when I realized the clock was ticking. She'd said she couldn't stay long so I threw out my next question. "Is Saxby going to be okay? The way my dreams end so far, I can't tell," and I picked up the bottle and pulled out the cork. Granny took a step closer and pulled out the chair farthest from me and sat down. I could see concern all over her face. She must've realized how much these dreams were bothering me.

"Oh dear, with our help he's going to be just fine, and believe it or not, things are going to turn out just hunky dory for Jackson too," and she gave me a warm Granny smile. "I've stopped your dreams, Cherry. You won't have another one like that after tonight, I promise you," and I watched as her eyes left mine and moved to the staircase. I turned, following her gaze. Brad was sitting on the third step down, watching us, sitting perfectly still. I smiled and looked back at my grandmother.

"How is Spanks, Granny? Is there any way you can bring him to visit the next time you come?"

I watched as her head dropped slowly downward and she looked at the floor. "Spanks has crossed over, Cherise," she said. There was a pause as her eyes closed, and then she looked at me with her lips thinned into a tight smile.

My heart felt as though it was being crushed. My legs suddenly felt rubbery. I felt glued to my chair, unable to move. But I didn't cry. I gave myself a moment before I asked, "But I thought you said Spanks was with you?" in a solemn tone; my disappointment seeping out. Her face lit up and I could see she wanted to assure me that Spanks' crossing was a positive thing. She must have wanted to go with him rather than stay behind.

"Dear, he was, but he's gone now. I hope to be joining him real soon." The thought of him being alone without Granny to watch over him was most upsetting, and I believe now she must have sensed that, or she'd read my mind. Maybe both.

"Cherise, he left the day you and Gene brought your two new doggies home from the rescue. He knew you'd be okay, and he wasn't sad. He was happy that you gave those two babies a new home where they'd feel just as loved and cared for as he had, until it's their time to cross over. That's what every dog yearns for. Please don't be sad," and just as those last four words touched my ears, my eyes filled and tears trickled down my cheeks. I really just wanted to kiss him one last time. I wiped my face and when I looked up at my grandmother, she was standing, so I stood too. I didn't want her to leave, not yet. I watched as she adjusted her towel and then looked over at Brad.

"Cherise, I have to ask you one thing that's really puzzling me dear," and I turned and watched Brad as he took one step at a time down the stairs. When he was sitting safely on the bottom step, I turned back to her.

"What's puzzling you, Granny?" and I watched her brow furrow and her expression turn serious. "Is it just me, or is one of those dogs you adopted the ugliest Dachshund that ever was?" I felt a chuckle bubble up from my chest and I couldn't help smiling.

"Granny, she's a Chihuahua, not a Dachshund," I told her. Relief rushed over the seriousness on her face and she smiled back at me.

"Thank goodness," she laughed. "I thought maybe it was because she was so ugly that Gene was being so protective," and she turned to walk over to the bottom step where Brad was sitting so patiently. I watched her bend over and give him a pat on the head, followed by, "Good boy" before she looked back at me. "It's time for me to go now, sweetie, but I promise to be back soon. We'll need Gene's sister, Jocelyn's help with this Jackson mess, when the time comes; but I'll leave all of that information in another dream real soon." I'm sure I was seeing things, but her cheeks looked just as rosy as they ever had. I wanted to run over and hug her, but I wasn't sure if that was possible, so I remained still.

"Oh Cherise, I'm no angel, I'm more like a glorified fairy godmother. And although you can see me, I'm still a ghost of sorts, but believe me, if I could hug you right now, I surely would. Unfortunately that's not possible. I'll try and better explain the rules I have to follow on my next trip, I promise. It'll make all of this a little easier for you to understand," and then a look of panic filled her face. "Charlotte's at it again, I've got to go now," and she blew me a kiss, followed by a big smile. "I love you, Cherry," and she was gone.

Brad and I stared at the trail of smoke as it rose toward the ceiling. It was several moments before the reality of it sank in. I'd just seen my grandmother. Suddenly Brad ran for the back door, for what looked to be a much-needed potty break. I reached for the bag of chips, my stomach growling in anticipation and sat on the back porch as the light from the full moon, shone brightly. I ate chips and watched as Brad stood in the yard among the shadows of the crisp morning, sniffing the air like a wild rabbit. My loud crunching sounds were the music for my private celebration of the end of that horrible dream.

Before I realized it, the little short-haired red guy was licking the back of my hand. I bent over and picked him up, cuddling him close to my chest before touching my nose to his cold wet one. I hugged him tightly for several moments, and then one more time for Spanks. I sat stroking his long muscular body until his head lifted and he gave me a quick surprise French kiss. I kissed the top of his head, squeezed his little body again, and whispered into his long droopy ear, "We have two guardian angels,

Brad. They're both kind of small, and kind of funny, but they're

all ours."

Chapter Ten
A Tale Of Two Mothers

Saturday, August 4, 2012

I felt the mattress sag as Gene lay down behind me, his arms enfolding me in a protective embrace. *He must have been up working on our website,* I thought in my sleepy fog. It had to be early, and with one eye open, I could see no sun peeking in from the slats of the window blinds. I yawned and stretched, arching my back into my husband's torso. I sighed with relief, glad the dream I'd had for the past two weeks had ceased. Nothing again last night.

"Go back to sleep," Gene whispered in my ear.

I rolled over to see Tomorrow's head lying in the space between Gene's head and shoulder. Up went a brow while the other held still, suggesting her displeasure at my moving. Gene couldn't see her, but there was a huge grin on his face; he knew her ways. She was black and tan, but the tan was more of a chestnut brown. She had little markings above her eyes; eyebrows as Gene called them, that she used to maneuver perfectly, to express herself. I'd never had a Chihuahua before, and her facial expressions were much easier to read than the doxies' faces. She had definitely adopted Gene as her *person*. She loved me too, but I was down a notch in her pecking order. She continued to rest on Gene's neck, holding her ground while her brown eyes stared into mine. A tiny tremor went through her body as she patiently waited for me to back away from her daddy. I laughed, lifting myself up, kissing Gene on the cheek before resting my nose on hers. She countered my attack by licking my face with wet kisses; her final warning for me to back off. Then Gene was laughing, and everyone moved up from the bottom of the bed to get a piece of the action. I glanced at the clock, it's hands pointing to the twelve and the five and I knew at this point, after being besieged with playful pooches, going back to sleep wasn't going to happen.

"Just lie still," Gene said as I rolled over to avoid his grasping fingers. Standing over him and the sea of weenies, all riled up and ready to start the day, I waited as each one made its way down the ramp and safely to the floor. Ryan was first to the door because he walks like he's being chased, and everyone else was in a tight line behind him, except the princess. She cracked me up. Her little ritual of turning, turning, turning and then plopping herself down next to Gene's head and tucking her wee head into her chest made me smile every time.

"Get some sleep," I mumbled over my shoulder and headed downstairs with the troops.

I opened the back door and turned on the outside light before racing for the downstairs bathroom. I rarely got to use it without a herd of escorts; a price you pay when you're adored by Dachshunds. After everyone had pottied, they followed me in and to the refrigerator where I grabbed a couple hotdogs. Six little butts wiggled, tails sweeping the floor in anticipation, while I divided the meat six ways. Each got a nibble before heading back up the staircase to rejoin their pack leader in that nice warm bed. They had their priorities.

As I poured myself a cup of coffee, I was reminded by the note hanging on the fridge that I was going to make potato salad for the birthday party the next day at Gene's parents home. In Gene's family there were so many kids, seven total; and when you added the spouses and grandkids, they'd resorted to having one big party once a month, and it was always a bring-a-dish potluck event. I'd become famous for Granny's potato salad. Gene's parents were not rich by any means. They'd scrimped and saved, wanting the best for their children, like so many other parents.

If one of the children wanted to go to college, Gene's parents found a way. This meant that Thomas Edward, or Eddy as he liked to be called, was out of town more than he was home; pretty much leaving Jasmine Lily, or Jazzy, a single mother.

No one in Gene's family ever complained, at least not that I'd ever heard, and I'd been part of the family a long time. Gene said his mom kept everyone too busy to complain. Jazzy was always at the top of her game. With Eddy away, she'd run her household better than any marine I'd ever met, and I'd met a few over my lifetime. She made my dad look like a cream puff.

She was petite and attractive but with an aura of strength. Nobody ever looked at her and said, *Oh, poor woman.* She dripped with confidence and authority. She was the super glue that held the Cones family together. When Gene had asked me to marry him, she called and invited me to lunch; telling me how happy she was to have a seventh daughter. I'd lucked out in the mother-in-law department. I knew it. Thinking about her just then made me feel a twinge of jealousy and guilt.

I'd spoken to my mother a handful of times by telephone since Gene and I had seen her in Truckee, watching Granny's burial from a distance. Neither of us had mentioned it. I wasn't altogether sure my mother knew that we knew she'd been there; although Gene swears she did. He thought we weren't hearing from her more because with Michael and me learning about Dustin being our biological father and then my father unable to forgive her and moving out, any fight she'd had left had literally fizzled out. Then add her mother's passing to that, and she'd just become paralyzed, realizing she'd sunk to the bottom of her personal fish bowl and there was nowhere else to go but up. He thought all this drama was somehow going to make her a better human being. He was a huge believer in miracles and could be extremely theatrical when it came to visualizing. He saw the healing potential of drama and was a big fan of miracles and happy endings.

My sister had given us her latest mom update the previous week, reporting that when she'd stopped over with the kids to visit, she'd asked my mom how she could have possibly not allowed her children to know their "real" father. She felt she'd witnessed humiliation spreading from the top of my mother's head to the tips of her toes. My sis could be blunt.

Now with thoughts of my sister, my mind switched gears to the dreams I'd had about my nephew. I took my coffee into the living room and sat on the sofa, searching my purse for my phone. My mind went into overdrive; conjuring up different scenarios, mostly all bad. I punched in Heather's number just as my eyes focused on the wall clock across the room. It was five-thirty in the morning. *No Cherry, this isn't the right time, and it's a bad idea.* Granny's face flashed before my eyes. I squelched the thought and punched *end*, tossing the phone back into my purse. There'd be plenty of opportunity later in the day. I put my empty coffee cup in the sink, tiptoed upstairs, reclaimed my side of the bed, and quickly fell asleep.

Chapter Eleven
Granny's Famous Potato Salad

When I finally awoke and looked around the room, it was empty. Gene and the dogs were gone. My husband's handsome face floated into my mind and I smiled. *He'd let me sleep in.* Feeling almost sleepier than I had the first time I'd awakened, I shimmied into a pair of pants I'd dropped on the floor the night before and followed the aroma of strong coffee wafting up from downstairs. As I made my journey to the kitchen, I peeked out the window to see Dachshunds sprawled out on the lawn, sunbathing on their backs, most showing teeth like a bunch of beached land sharks, except for the Chihuahua. She was standing between Gene's legs like a little ankle ornament.

"Well good morning, Miss Bed-Head, love of my life," he said and grinned my way, pouring the coffee. I might have responded sarcastically if I'd had my wits about me. Sitting at the table, a cup of coffee in front of me, I looked down at Tomorrow.

"Why isn't she outside enjoying the sunshine with the rest of them?" I asked.

"She was," Gene said quickly, "but I wanted to take a few pictures of her without her bros and sistas all up in her grill. That's why she's in here," he added with a lip pop. I'd seen several of his previous attempts to get that *perfect* picture. Tomorrow would shiver as she posed for a picture Gene was determined to take. She always looked like she was terrified; as if somewhere in her past she'd had an awful photo shoot experience. We would probably never know but Gene wasn't ready to throw away the camera just yet. She would be the star model in many more photos before her portfolio was complete.

"So, can she quit for the day?" I questioned jokingly.

"Yeah, I actually have to go over to the storage unit and pick up some merchandise for orders going out on Monday. I boiled some potatoes for you, too," he said, glancing at the colander in the sink. "And I've wrapped all the gifts for the party tomorrow." That last word garnered the attention of the little dog and her front paws started tapping the floor anxiously in excited response. Gene often bought all the gifts for his family online, and then wrapped them, so when the gifts were received, it was a total surprise for me, too.

Granny's No Angel 66

"Thank you," I said, gripping my coffee cup with both hands.

"Do you need me to go with you?" I asked, seriously hoping he didn't.

"No, I actually know where everything is this time," he announced proudly. His eyes were focused on something behind me. Following his gaze, I turned to see the light on the answering machine blinking. I blew out a heavy sigh.

"You go, and I'll check it," I offered. Clearly delighted, he scooped up the little Chi, herded the weenies into the house and then into the car. We knew the only two people who ever called the house phone were my mom and Heather.

As I listened to the garage door slam shut, I poured myself another cup of coffee and began gathering the ingredients for Granny's famous potato salad, which follows:

Nolte's Famous Potato Salad

5 pounds, clean, scrubbed red potatoes
2 cups mayonnaise
½ cup kosher dill pickle juice
2 lg. sweet onions, finely chopped
1½ cups chopped celery
½ cup mild cheddar cheese, shredded
5 kosher dill pickles, finely chopped
5 boiled eggs, chopped
1 tsp garlic salt
3 teaspoons prepared mustard
1 small jar of pimentos
Smoked paprika

Directions

Bring a large pot of salted water to a boil. Add the potatoes and cook until tender but still firm, about 15-20 minutes. Drain, place in a large mixing bowl, and dice. Add all other ingredients and toss. Refrigerate overnight.

Just before serving, garnish with leaves from the celery stalks and sprinkle with smoked paprika.

Chapter Twelve
Good News And A Bad Odor

Wednesday, August 8, 2012

The call on the answering machine had been from my mother, and I'd not called her back. It did prompt me to call Mr. Gretsky first thing the following Monday. Mom had finally caught wind that Michael wasn't going to be moving into Granny's house and she'd stated in her message that she was worried about the house being left empty. She had a point. Because Mr. Gretsky had been in court the day I called, his secretary assured me he'd get back to me in the next few days. His call this morning, gave us a lot to ponder.

He reminded us that Granny had left the house to Gene and me with the provision that Michael could rent it, giving us the income to pay the yearly property taxes and homeowners insurance. The money from the auction sale was to be spent on new, modern furnishings for the house. With my brother's recent decision to move in with Dustin, Gene and I had some major decisions to make. And then there was the dreaded chore of informing my mother of our newest discovery about the legal ownership of Granny's house. She wasn't going to be a happy camper. My aunts and uncle probably weren't going to be thrilled with the news either.

Gene and I were perplexed with my grandmother's decision, and I wanted to speak to her about it more than ever. Although it was a sweet gesture on her part, another piece of property to worry about and maintain could prove to be more daunting than rewarding. She must've had her reasons, and in that moment I truly wished I understood what they were. I knew there was no chance Michael would change his mind about renting Granny's, or I guess *our* house now, because I'd spoken to Dustin on Sunday evening.

He'd been excited about the way Michael's life seemed to have taken a one-hundred-eighty degree turn. He was doing normal *life* stuff. There were no more late nights out at the bars and strange women or irresponsible decisions. He was going to work, coming home, contributing to the daily chores, and taking care of his children on the weekends. Translated, he was actually acting like an adult. It wasn't that I didn't believe Dustin; it was more a personal issue I had with myself. I'm the type of person who has to see it to believe it; and in my book, not enough time had passed to give him bragging rights. As Granny used to say, *you can put lipstick on a pig, but it's still a pig.* And some people just love to exaggerate. Dustin was happy to finally have that boy he'd always wanted. I got that. But for now, the only thing that Gene and I were positive about was his and Michael's new bro-mance wasn't helping us with our new-house dilemma. We needed to figure out a feasible plan, and quickly. The taxes and insurance on my grandmother's house weren't going to pay themselves.

Gene went up to take a shower and I tidied up around the house. Our plan was to stop by Mr. Gretsky's office, pick up the check from the sale and then swing by the house and do a quick walk-through. We hadn't been there for awhile. As I finished cleaning the kitchen, Gene barreled down the stairs, dressed, but his hair was still visibly wet; it was dripping. Following close behind him was the gang. When Gene ran, they ran; when he stopped, they stopped. Last in line was the Chihuahua. She needed three steps to each one of the doxies.

"So when do you want to head out?" he asked just as he cleared the last step, "and is this a dog or no-dog trip?" he added. I turned and stared at him and his loyal herd of tiny jesters. Gene shook his head like a dog getting a bath.

"Uhmm, you're getting water everywhere. And no dogs this trip." My eyes narrowed.

"Okay guys, mom says you must stay and guard the castle today. Let's go out and potty" and they bounded out through the back door. Another fifteen minutes for Gene to get his hair combed and sprayed, clothes primped and tucked, and we were finally out the door and on our way. Some days it just doesn't seem fair that your husband is prettier than you.

When we arrived at the lawyer's office, I ran in while Gene hung at the curb in front of the building. A sealed letter with our name written on the front was waiting for me at the front desk. Once back in the car, Gene's eyes were glued to the envelope in my hand.

"So, how much is it?" he asked, extremely interested.

"I haven't looked yet; just drive," but the car didn't move. When I looked up at the wide-eyed innocence on his face, I caved. That look did it to me every time.

"I'm almost afraid to look," I admitted. Gene held out his hand, and I placed the unopened envelope in it. "That was my grandmother's life they sold at that auction," I said; more to myself than to him. I watched as he ripped the envelope open. "Is it bad?" I asked, watching him intensely.

He went all serious and wasn't giving me any answers. He was reading down the page carefully, examining the breakdown of all the money that had been spent for the auction house's costs and taxes until finally I saw a huge smile cover his face. "It's good, Cherry; very, very good," he said triumphantly.

I grabbed the paper from him and followed the printed figures down the page until I reached the final set of numbers; eleven-thousand one-hundred-thirty-six dollars and fifty-four cents. I looked back at Gene in silence, my eyes widened.

"That's a miracle," he said. "Your grandmother's furniture was old and maybe there were a few antiques but most of it was just odds and ends. To get that kind of money after paying all the auction house's costs is nothing short of a small miracle."

I looked into his eyes while I tried to wrap my brain around everything he'd just said. "I don't believe in miracles. You know that," and I quickly folded the letter and placed it back into the envelope with the check.

The ride to Granny's house was only ten minutes away, but for some reason, it felt more like an hour-long trip. It was five-fifteen in the evening and traffic was thick. Going back to see the house empty wasn't something I relished.

When we arrived, Gene unlocked the front door and held it open for me. I was about three steps in before I noticed a terrible stench in the room and fought the urge to lift my fingers to my nose. Gene had stopped at the door. It was as if the smell had paralyzed him. As I moved deeper into the house, my eyes searched every wall, trying to determine where the odor was coming from. I completed the full circle through the house and met Gene back at the front door. He was standing with one foot on the front porch, waving me out of the house. It was that bad. I stepped outside.

Granny's No Angel 74

"Something definitely died in there, Cherise," he said. I took in several gulps of fresh air and looked back into the house. "It smells like a dozen skunks dropped dead in there," he added.

"I didn't see anything that would cause such a foul stench. There's nothing in there," I assured him.

"Maybe something got up in the attic, or down in the basement, he offered with a shrug. The cool breeze tickled the back of my neck, raising the hair on my arms.

My thoughts were scattered. What could've gotten into a locked house and died in the last two weeks? It just didn't make any sense. I looked up at Gene. I knew the last thing he wanted to do was to go looking for something dead in an empty house. As the minutes ticked by, a hint of pleading was obvious in those gorgeous brown eyes. He wanted to get the heck out of there.

"So, let's lock up and I'll call Mr. Gretsky tomorrow. Maybe he knows someone who could come by and check it out for us," I said. I couldn't have beaten Gene to the van if I'd tried.

Chapter Thirteen
A Surprise Visit

Saturday, August 11, 2012

I woke up at six-thirty to the sound of honking coming from the street out front. The fan, which usually provided white noise, and blocked sounds of cars passing by outside our bedroom window, must have been off. As my eyes began to focus, I jumped, and then let out a blood-curdling shriek. Two old women's beady eyes were staring at me, just inches from my face. They then giggled like two school children, apparently pleased that they had scared me. I turned over and looked at Gene; he was out cold, and obviously had not heard my scream. *Comforting*, I thought.

They'd been kneeling by the side of my bed, for who knows how long, waiting for me to wake up. As I sat up, I realized that all seven of the dogs were staring at Granny and the strange woman who I guessed was Charlotte. So it wasn't just me; they were clearly able to see them, too. The dogs looked like statues. They just sat staring, almost trance-like, at our two visitors. No one moved a muscle. It was almost mystifying. I really wanted to know how they did that statue trick. It might prove to be very handy some day.

As I made my way down the hallway, both ladies followed until we reached the staircase, then they swished past me and into the kitchen. There was daylight, yet the house was still fairly dark with all the curtains still closed. I opened the refrigerator and grabbed the jug of orange juice, secretly wishing there was some vodka to pour into it. No such luck. When I turned back to the ladies, it hit me. Maybe this was a dream, or worse, the twilight zone. Granny had never come during the day, only in the middle of the night when it was dark.

"You're not dreaming, Cherise," my grandmother said softly; a little embarrassment in her voice.

"Oh crap," I mumbled back, remembering that she could read my thoughts, and immediately wrapped my arms around my body in an attempt to cover myself. For a moment, I felt vulnerable. "Dear, I can't see under your clothes, only what you're thinking," she snickered. The woman next to her stared back at me with a stern look on her face, making me feel as if this visit was keeping her from places she'd much rather be.

Granny's No Angel 77

She was taller than Granny, her hair was cut short, and she was wearing a lime-green pantsuit. Trying not to stare, I noticed napkins stuffed into and overflowing from all of her pockets. *That's odd*, I thought, before I could stop myself. My grandmother shot me a look, followed by a big grin.

"We all call her the napkin Nazi," Her voice was humorous and her eyes twinkled. "She's my cross to bear," and then Charlotte's eyes were on Granny.

"You said this was just going to be a quick stop, Rose," she spat, followed by a muffled curse. Hearing the tone she was using with my grandmother was infuriating, but I managed to bite my tongue.

"If you'll just hold your horses, dear Grambo, I'll say what I came to say and we can be on our way," and she glanced back my way, revealing her fatigue with the whole Charlotte baby-sitting situation.

I sat down in a chair, my eyes lingering on both women.

"Tomorrow, late afternoon, you'll get a call from either your mother or Heather, whoever has the fastest dialing finger, I suppose," and she squared her shoulders and straightened to her full height of five-feet-some-inches. "I'm going to leave you a little movie of sorts, a dream really; to give you more information tonight, so no wine tonight, Cherise. It's really important that you use everything you're able to remember when you awaken. You'll need to have your wits about you" and her tone of voice was meant to chastise. Something admittedly, that I'd had very little experience with. She was trying to convey that this was going to be extremely important. I got what Granny was putting down even if I was confused at what her warning really meant.

"So how will I know what to do?" I blurted out. "And you have my back, right? You're going to help me if I need it, right?"

Before Granny could answer me, Charlotte pipe up. "Rose," and she pointed to something that clearly intrigued her. I looked in the direction of where her finger was pointing and there sat six little Dachshunds and one tiny, shivering Chihuahua. In a perfectly-orchestrated line, each occupying a step on the staircase, their eyes shone, but as before, not one of them flexed a muscle. They could've been little doggy mannequins or maybe even stuffed toys. "I really miss my little dog," Charlotte said finally. Granny turned to the woman and gave her a sweet smile.

"I know, Char, and we'll stop over and visit with her as soon as we leave here. You have my word."

"And then back to Vegas?" she asked, with a big grin.

"Yes, then back to Elvis and bingo land," my grandmother cheerfully replied. Hearing the answer she wanted, Charlotte turned her attention back to the dogs. I stood and tried to think of any questions I might need answers to before the napkin Nazi demanded that they leave.

"So, the old dream about Saxby being kidnapped and held in a dark room and the dream that I will have tonight, together, will help me find him when he goes missing?"

My grandmother nodded.

"So if we already know this is going to happen, wouldn't it be better just to stop it now? Why can't we nip it in the bud and save everyone all the worrying?" I questioned. I could see from the look on her face that I was asking things she couldn't answer, and before I could think of another question, Charlotte interrupted with a snap.

"She can't tell you that, child. That's not how it works," she announced rudely. I sucked in a breath through clenched teeth and sat down in my chair. The look on my grandmother's face told me I needed to be patient. That would prove way easier said than done.

Chapter Fourteen
She Was Right

Monday, August 13, 2012

It was seven-thirty in the evening and I decided to take a bath after a long day of running household-related errands and mailing out store orders with Gene. There was a rare summer storm and it had rained off and on all day, and although I never minded driving, at times the rain had actually pelted the windshield, making it difficult to see and inevitably, I had a miserable headache I couldn't seem to shake. The two Tylenol I'd taken weren't even touching it. After dinner, my head was still pounding and after taking two more Tylenol, I announced to Gene that a quiet bath might be the ticket.

As I made my way up the stairs, I heard Gene yell from the living room sofa, "Stay golden, pony-boy" and I smiled; I knew exactly which movie he and the pups were watching. My pace increased; anticipating some much-needed *me* time. The hot water felt wonderful and soothing. My mind began to relax; a calmness settled over me. Before long I was having the same dream I'd had weeks earlier; the one Granny had assured me would end. I awakened in cold water; prune-like fingers, and goose bumps all over my body. I sighed with relief that the horrible dream was over. As I stepped out of the tub, a chilling thought came over me. *What if Granny had been wrong? What if she didn't have as much power as she thought she had? She was new at this. What if she couldn't control this bad scenario that was about to play out with Saxby?*

I cringed at the memory of what I'd seen happen again and again in my dream. I grabbed a nightgown and as I slipped it on, I eyed the perfectly empty bed and laid down.

Two things were eating at me. Well, three really. First, Granny had said a new dream would replace the bad one and it hadn't. Next, she'd told me we were going to need Gene's sister, Jocelyn, to help us when the time came. I couldn't very well ask her for help when I had no clue as to what we would need her to do. We'd attended the Cones family birthday celebration yesterday as planned, but didn't stay long, as usual, because we'd left all the dogs at home. Well, except for Tomorrow. A picket fence circles Gene's parents home, and yep, it's white. Jazzy has beautiful, prize-winning rose bushes scattered throughout the perfectly-manicured yard. A yard that definitely isn't doxie friendly. Since Eddy retired, the yard has been his responsibility, and he's stuck very close to his wife and their home, probably in an effort to make up for all the time spent traveling during his career.

Gene finally found a place to park, a half-block away. I grabbed the potato salad and deviled eggs while Gene unbuckled our spoiled-rotten Chihuahua from her car seat. When the Cones family has a family gathering, parking is always scarce. Once inside, I counted all six sisters, a few of their husbands, and a herd of little people strewn about the house. Gene's mom appeared suddenly; first hugging her son before giving the little dog in his arms a tender rubbing behind her ears. With a smile and a peck on Jazzy's cheek, I headed for the kitchen to add our dishes to the already-huge food smorgasbord. Of all of Gene's sisters, Alice Marie, the oldest daughter of the Cones family, is probably my favorite. At 44, she is shy; the shortest of her siblings, wears glasses, and has the oddest cowlick in the middle of her hairline. It reminds me of the circular spot on Angelina's butt; probably the reason she uses so much gel on her hair.

Jocelyn Topaz, 42, the second oldest and maybe my least favorite of all Gene's sisters, spotted me and reached out, giving me her usual awkward, one-armed hug, with a quick tap on my back as a finish. She's the private investigator; the one I'm supposed to ask for help. Her dark auburn hair frames her oval-shaped, flawless face, while her long black lashes compliments her chocolate-brown eyes. Her cheeks are perfectly blushed, giving her the appearance of a highly-paid model. Her clothes look expensive and who knows how many pairs of shoes she owns. She's pretty much the female version of my husband. Her biggest fault? She isn't fond of animals and she isn't shy about letting people know. *Am I jealous of her*? Honestly, there are days when I'm not feeling as good as I could about myself, and just as oil and water don't mix, my insecurities make me feel less than adequate. I think everyone knows someone who does that to them. Jocelyn is the fly in my ointment, as Granny would say.

Gene's other sisters are all pretty grounded and down-to-earth; normal. Kimberly Kristina, 41, is known for her brutal honesty, and I like that about her. She is also the daughter with the most offspring. Summer, I don't remember her middle name, is 40 and has one child, conceived from a sperm donor. She doesn't believe in marriage, it's just a piece of paper, she rants. Although I don't always agree with her reasoning on certain issues; she has a genuine warmth and kindness that radiates from within, like steam from a billowing tea kettle.

Suzanne JoAnne, 38, well; all I can say about her is that she has the uncanny ability to make anyone blush. When she speaks, it's almost as if her mouth and brains are somehow totally disconnected, until she notices the look on your face. Our first meeting was years ago, but I remember it as if it were yesterday. "Hi, I'm Suzy. I'm the sister who has to drink an entire bottle of wine before I can give myself one of those self-breast exams." I remember I just stood and stared, my mouth hanging open, trying to get the words I thought I'd heard to register. Gene still teases me about it. She never fails to come up with some real mind benders. Our dogs all love her so I let her oddness slide.

Debbie Lee, 37, the baby of the girls, has the ability to laugh at anything, and I mean *anything*. It's entertaining for the first hour or two, but then it becomes annoying. Once, in confidence, and she swore me to secrecy, while at a family dinner at Red Lobster, she and I went to the ladies' room together and she claimed that every relationship she'd ever had was in some way sabotaged by one of her older siblings. I wanted to say that maybe it was because her laughing at everything was annoying, but I managed to hold my tongue. She and Gene aren't all that close, and Jazzy explained to me when I first joined the family that she feels it's because they're both "the babies". She did that quotation thing in the air to emphasize her words. I get along fine with her, but Gene and Debbie have never been more than cordial. The night ended well and we returned home with two empty dishes and our pint-sized furry princess.

The last thing gnawing at me was that Mr. Gretsky hadn't returned my call about investigating the stench at Granny's house. It had been several days with no word from either him or his secretary.

"Cherry, are you awake, baby?" Gene's voice was quiet and calm. For several moments I wasn't sure if it was morning or night. The blinds were closed so the room was very dark. *Why had he let me sleep?*

Before I had time to ask him, he added, "Heather's downstairs and she's really upset. Saxby's gone missing and they've looked everywhere and can't find him."

My eyes flew open and I leapt out of bed. I reached for the lamp and as the light landed on Gene's face, I could see his eyes were open wide, his pupils dilated, and he looked as though the wind had been knocked out of him. He was more than concerned. "Damn it, she was right," I whispered to myself.

Chapter Fifteen
The Reality Sets In

When we got to the living room, my sister was sitting on the far left side of the sofa, closest to the front door. Gene disappeared outside to bring the dogs in from the yard, closing the kiddie gate behind him. Looking at my sister, I noticed several things immediately. Instead of looking at me, she began digging in her purse until she came up with a half-empty bag of corn chips. Pouring some in her hand and popping them into her mouth, she chewed, her cheeks bulging as she finally looked at me.

"What the hell is going on, Heather?" I asked, as I waited patiently for her to finish chewing. She was obviously considering her words. She could yank Gene's chain with the whole damsel-in-distress routine but she knew I wasn't a push-over. I read her like a book. I'm sure a full minute had elapsed and I could feel the heat rising in my cheeks. My stomach began to churn, and within seconds my heart was galloping; my palms felt clammy. I could see snippets of my dream flashing in my head, but it was like a fading black-and-white picture show with cloudy-gray images.

Saxby was crying and calling out for someone, anyone, to find him. Finally I stomped my foot in frustration. Heather dropped the bag into her purse and looked me in the eye.

"Jackson took Sax to work with him today as he does at least twice a week maybe, only today he wandered off while his dad was with a customer out on the lot. We've searched the car lot and even the route he'd take if he walked home, but we can't find him anywhere." I was speechless as I watched her hand reach down into her purse for the chip bag. She broke eye contact and poured the remaining chips into her mouth. As she wadded up the empty bag, I could only gawk at her, stupefied. Her nonchalant manner infuriated me.

"And you're sitting in my living room, rather than looking for him, because? Have you called the police to report him missing?" I felt Gene's hands settle on my hips from behind. Maybe to hold me back, I'm not completely sure. I glanced at him and then shifted impatiently from one foot to the other as my irritation mounted.

"Heather, how long has he been gone and where's Jackson?" I spat. Before she could answer, the kitchen phone rang and I jumped. Gene and I ignored it as we waited for my sister to answer my question. We knew it had to be my mother. Gene released his hold on me, but flinched when it rang again. As he left the room to answer the phone, I moved closer to Heather. She shifted her weight, crossing and uncrossing her arms, probably wishing that I'd stop staring at her.

"Cherry, Jackson has assured me that he'll find our son. He says this is just some elaborate prank that some guys he knows are playing on him. He said I shouldn't worry and Sax will be home safe and sound. He's probably somewhere eating too much ice cream and having the time of his life with Jackson's friends," and then her eyes left mine and focused on Gene, behind me. With the phone to his ear, his eyes were glued to mine while he spoke. "Yep, I'll relay the message," he said as he turned and headed back to the kitchen.

When Gene opened the gate, Tomorrow squeezed her little body through and ran past him as he tried to corral everyone else into the kitchen. She ran past me and jumped up on the sofa next to my sister. I crouched, creeping to the sofa to retrieve her, and as I put both hands on the furry ball of spunk, the startled dog let out a yelp and I sat down with her in my lap, next to Heather.

I looked into my sister's face and the only thing I could wonder was *why she wasn't paralyzed with fear if she believed that someone she didn't even know had her child. How could she take Jackson's word that everything was okay?* Because of my dreams, I *was* paralyzed with fear. And maybe it was me making more of the situation than was really necessary. Granny had said it was all going to work out. Why couldn't I just trust her words to be true? Instead, I was letting my emotions cloud any real help I could offer to rectify this awful situation that was really actually happening and help my grandmother move to that pickle position she so much wanted. Tomorrow placed her front paws on my chest and I endured a hot, wet, slimy face-licking before Gene was able to rescue his furry little girl from my arms. As he took her back to the kitchen, I turned to my sister and saw her organic mascara making wavy trails down both sides of her face. I felt bad, so I placed a reassuring hand on her arm.

"Heather, I can't put my finger on it but something's just not right about this picture. I think Jackson knows more about all
Granny's No Angel 92

of this than he's telling you. It makes me nauseous to say this, but I almost think he might somehow be involved," I admitted, with genuine fear.

I knew he was involved but there was only so much I could tell my sister. *Our dead grandmother, whom we both know was buried in Truckee, showed up in my kitchen while I was drinking wine one night and warned me that Saxby was going to be kidnapped and your husband was involved.* Uh-uh, instead, "I'm not sure how I know, but I can just feel it. His story seems too perfect." My sister's face was almost frozen into a comical expression, as if she were processing what I'd just said and was waiting for the punch line to a horrible joke. I heard Gene clear his throat. He was standing five feet from us and had *that look* on his face. The one that said I wasn't going to be happy with the news.

"Your mom's over at Heather's house with the kids, and Jackson, Dustin and Michael are on their way over here." He was right. I didn't relish the thought of seeing Jackson right then.

Chapter Sixteen
What Now

Tuesday, August 14, 2013

It was after midnight before anyone actually arrived at our house. Thirty minutes before the doorbell rang, Heather called me into the bathroom for a chat; for what I totally thought was going to be a *be-nice-to- Jackson* lecture. Nothing could've prepared me for the words she shared. Things in my life were becoming more and more outlandish. It was almost as if a gray-haired woman in her flannel nightgown was sitting at her computer, writing a crazy fiction novel, and my dysfunctional family and I were the main characters. Unbeknownst to me, my sister had secretly had a DNA test done, curious about whether she too might be a product of my mother's infidelities. I vaguely remember her asking me if I'd be down with taking something of Dustin's for her to have tested, but at the time I assumed she was joking and just laughed it off. She'd taken a paper cup that our dad, Harry, had used during a visit with him at the zoo with her kids. *How very Colombo of her*, I thought.

"So....about Dustin," she smiled nervously, putting a strand of blonde hair behind her ear. My back was flush against the

Granny's No Angel 94

closed door. Stone-faced and still kind of upset with her, I looked straight into her face. Several minutes passed, and she just sat on the commode, staring up at me with blue eyes and glossy pink lips. The silence was making me insane. We were in there so she could tell me something, not the other way around.

"So," I finally replied, and her expression informed me without bothering with the words. My eyes flew wide, "No way," I scoffed. "That's just redic," I watched as she rubbed her temples with her left hand before looking back at me.

"Michael got me something of Dustin's to have tested and it came back ninety-nine-point-nine percent positive, and he is my biological father."

I leaned forward; my balance was wobbly, but an involuntary grin split across my face. One of those faces you make when you're so flustered by something and you're not sure how else to react, and your face kinda does unexpected things.

"So Harry was just mom's test-dummy dad?" I said, my cheeks reddening as I listened to my own words. Heather lowered her eyes and pursed her lips in annoyance. It was blatantly clear that Dustin being *her* dad was not a welcome thing. I stepped back, my weight on the bathroom door. Eyes still glued to the floor, my sister continued and I listened without interrupting.

"Yeah, when you and Michael found out that Dustin was your real dad, I was actually thrilled with the news. For me, it meant that dad, Harry, was all mine" and without looking up at me, she grabbed a tissue from the box on the counter next to her. I slid down the door to a squatting position, hoping that she'd at least make eye contact with me, but she didn't. Just as my butt hit the floor, there was a knock on the door.

"Babe, are you okay?" Gene asked.

"Yeah, we're okay. In fact, I was just about ready to get Heather and I a glass of wine," I answered. He didn't respond but I could hear movement on the other side of the door. "Gene?" I pressed.

"Yeah, I heard you. I'm just rounding up the dogs to run them upstairs before they get here," and all I heard after that was a small short-legged army being beckoned by their leader.

"Anyway," she continued, "Mom, Granny, and Dad, pretty much everyone, has always treated you like their favorite and so I thought being Dad's only child would at least make me a shoe-in for him. Now, not so." She looked me square in the eye. "How did that thing go that Granny used to say? *Curiosity killed the cat?*" and she crumpled the tissue up to her nose.

"Yeah, *but satisfaction brought him back*," I piped in, hoping to make her smile. No dice.

"My point is that now I wish I'd never found out, just left it all alone. Now, when Harry finds out..." and she dropped her head into her hands.

"So, who actually knows that Dustin's your father?" I watched as she shrugged, but looked up at me.

"You, Michael, and me, I guess. Don't tell Gene," she demanded. Right then I should have spoken up and told her that that wasn't happening. Except for seeing my grandmother, and I mean actually seeing her, Gene knew everything.

"Good heavens, Cherry, everything in my life's going into the shitter." Her eyes dropped back to the floor. I sat silent, not moving, waiting for her to finish. "I know Jackson's done something really stupid and this time he's pissed off the wrong person, but he claims the things he's been doing were only to help our family. We're about to lose our house; another thing you don't need to be repeating to anyone."

"Of course not," I replied quickly. "Do you know what this stupid thing is?" I asked before she had a chance to continue. She cleared her throat and threw the tissue in the waste basket, as I watched. *Seriously*, I screamed silently.

"Do you think I'm ignorant? Of course, I know. Well, let's just say I know enough," and she cleared her throat again. The fact that she was sitting here in my bathroom talking about anything other than finding her twelve-year-old son was as wrong as wearing two left shoes.

I'd freak out if one of my dogs didn't come when I called, even if I absolutely knew it was somewhere in the safety of our house, not out in the world somewhere with people I don't know. I squeezed my eyes shut tightly, and then opened them quickly. *Nope. This wasn't just a bad dream.*

Evidently my sister had been talking while I'd quietly checked and evaluated my physical and psychological states, and I heard, "I'm not stupid, Cherise. I'm smart enough to home-school all four of my children." I tried to focus and catch up.

"I know Jackson went to Mr. Gretsky's office to see if it was possible for us to rent Granny's house, since Michael had moved in with Dustin. And I know that Jackson had the key to her house because I found an empty envelope with her address written on the outside and a clear key impression on it from his pants pocket. I know he's taken *something*, and I swear to you, I have no clue what, and hidden it somewhere in her house."

I couldn't help but cringe when she mentioned my grandmother's house. That awful smell permeated the premises as if something had died, and then the lawyer had not returned my call. Maybe he hadn't been able to get into the house if Jackson had the key. Maybe Jackson had stolen the key from his office. My mind did a back-flip. What had he hidden in that house that could have made it smell so wretched? When I finally looked back at my sister, she was pulling her knees to her chest, swinging her arms around them tightly, balancing her one-hundred-fifteen-pound frame on the toilet seat. I hadn't noticed but she'd also been crying; fresh mascara trails ran down her cheeks. I stood, grabbed a tissue from the box and handed it to her.

"Come on," I coaxed. "Let's go get that glass of wine."

Wine was not the wisest drink of choice at that moment, but it sounded better than sitting on the bathroom floor doing nothing. What did we need? Some kind of miracle I thought, or my grandmother materializing and telling me exactly what to do.

Chapter Seventeen
The Showdown

Gene was in the kitchen, tipping back in a chair, arms folded tightly across his chest, obviously waiting for us. My sister announced that she was going to go check her cell phone and I grabbed a bottle of wine from the fridge. As I searched the drawer for the corkscrew, Gene hefted himself up onto the countertop and watched as I attempted to remove the cork.

"So, what did you find out?" he asked as he took the bottle from me and quickly and easily removed the cork, handing me the opened bottle. I rolled my eyes as I poured the wine. Patient, strong and sexy; great qualities my husband possessed; all of which I treasured.

As we sat down at the kitchen table, I peeked into the living room to see Heather's back to me, phone to her ear, and I leaned into Gene and whispered, "Jackson has the key to Granny's house and Heather said that he's hidden something that he's taken from someone. She says that she doesn't know all the details, and I believe her." and Gene's brow furrowed as he turned to be sure that my sister wasn't coming.

"So how did he get the key?" he asked, with a confused look on his face.

"Beats me!" He must have stolen it from Mr. Gretsky's office; she said he went there to ask if they could rent the house since Michael wasn't going to. I guess they didn't get the memo that it's our house now. He was probably looking to get the kid's savings bonds too, who knows?" and I stopped as Gene's face froze. I swear I could see one of those little light bulbs come on above his head. He was slowly putting things together; but he wasn't ready to share it yet.

Then he almost squeaked out, "That could have been pot we smelled" his eyes getting bigger. I sat back, my hand tightening on the glass. I liked the feeling of the cool wine glass in my hand. The reality of it somehow reassured me that this wasn't just another bad dream. As we sat staring into each other's eyes, there was a knock on the front door. We didn't move, knowing that Heather was in the room; we thought she would answer it.

"Jackson's gotten himself involved with drug dealers," Gene whispered. Our mouths hung open as we pondered that theory. Finally I tipped the glass to my lips and guzzled down a half-glass of wine. Another knock.... loud and more urgent than the first. Gene jumped up and headed for the door, passing Heather who was sitting on the sofa as if she'd just decided to ignore the knocks. *She's picking now, of all times, to be upset with her husband,* I thought to myself, as I stood in the kitchen doorway. When Gene opened the door, Jackson was standing on the front porch.

"Let me talk to Heather," he demanded. Gene stepped aside, allowing my brother-in-law to enter. He walked straight over to her, and I could see he was squeezing something in his hand. He unclenched his fist and a white piece of paper fell to the floor. His breathing was labored; his face glistened; his hair was wet and matted against his head as if he'd just taken off a hat.

"I need you to come home," he scoffed. My sister shot me a glance and just let it settle, as if she'd not heard a word he'd said, and I wasn't sure if she was asking for privacy with her husband or begging me for help.

"Where's Saxby, Jackson?" I spoke up. Several moments later he turned from Heather and faced Gene and me.

"I have it handled," he said in a friendly tone. I didn't lash out at him the way I wanted to, and I honestly believe that I had that glass of wine to thank for that.

"Is this all about drugs?" and that last word filled me with dread. Minutes ago, in the kitchen, it had only been a crazy theory of Gene's. His answer was going to make it all very real.

"Are there drugs in my grandmother's house?" I asked. Jackson jerked his chin up at that, face flushed with *maybe* a sprinkle of genuine embarrassment that he'd been caught red-handed. *Maybe*.

"I goofed up, okay? I didn't think they'd go and take Sax," and his hands flew up and behind him as he cradled the back of his head.

"You goofed up, really?" Gene finally piped in. "That's the world's biggest understatement," he added.

"You need to tell us what you know about these friends of yours and you need to do it like yesterday, Jackson," I said, my tone calm and authoritative.

"Nope, you need to let me handle this. You can't help me," he said, shaking his head.

"Why not?" I asked, squaring myself for battle. I knew more about where Saxby was than he did. I'd seen that awful dream play out more times than I'd ever wanted to; and, I had validation, even if it was from my non-physical seventy-six-year-old grandmother.

"You're a real piece of work," Gene hissed.

Across the room, my sister was now standing. "I'm staying here. You'd better bring me my son, Jackson; and there'd better not be a scratch on him," I watched as she bit her lip; probably to stop it from trembling and clasped her shaking hands in front of her. "Oh Jackson," she whispered, "How could you have done this? How could you have put our family, our children, in jeopardy? And for what? So you could make some easy money? There is *always* another way." The look on her face was a combination of disappointment and disgust as she turned from him, and with a final glance my way, she went into the kitchen.

Jackson took two steps forward to follow, but Gene stepped back, barricading the kitchen doorway.

Granny's No Angel 105

"Jackson, you're an ass," and before I could stop myself, I added, "And my sister is way too good for the likes of your ass, you ass." The word *ass* and I were on a giant roll, but it felt good to finally say it out loud and to his face. He'd had it coming for years. He turned and marched to the front door, and my eyes searched the floor where I'd seen him drop the piece of paper. I hadn't seen him pick it up. Gene moved to close the front door behind him but he'd planted his foot on the threshold to stop the door from closing.

"Tell Heather to call me," and he turned and left.

"What happened to that paper?" I asked, perplexed. Gene and I searched the living room floor and the sofa, but it wasn't there. Heather must have gone upstairs while I was telling her husband off because we found the kitchen empty. I picked up my glass to place it in the sink and from the corner of my eye I saw it. She'd placed the paper on the kitchen table. It had several different names, maybe friends or co-workers. Two names were scratched out. I'd need my sister to help answer all the questions swimming in my head.

Gene came from behind me and wrapped his arms around my waist. "What the hell just happened?" he asked. I shrugged my shoulders and contemplated another glass of wine.

"So are we going to go find Saxby?" and I turned my body, grabbing his waist, and looked into his face.

"Maybe," I answered, but my eyes dropped to his chest as I mustered up the courage to say what I needed to say.

"We'll be like Bonnie and Clyde to the rescue," he said with a chuckle.

"Bonnie and Clyde were outlaws and they died," I reminded him.

"Okay, not my best analogy," he admitted.

Bringing my eyes back up to meet his, I took a deep breath. "Gene, I really need to tell you something and I want you to believe me, no matter how crazy it sounds. Promise me you won't think I'm crazy?"

Chapter Eighteen
Candle Light, Candle Bright

Honestly, how could I expect Gene not to think I was crazy when I wasn't even sure of it myself? His arms were wrapped around my waist, his brown eyes clearly soothing me, as he studied my face. I licked my lips, but my tongue was dry as I prepared myself for his reaction. He put his right-hand finger under my chin and pulled my face up to his; placing a gentle, reassuring kiss on my nose. I gulped a big breath of air and just as I began to force my words out, I saw a dark, motionless figure, beginning to materialize. My grandmother was standing behind him, just over his shoulder. Our eyes met and I froze; my legs suddenly felt like rubber, and I'd have collapsed if Gene hadn't held me so tightly. "Whoa, are you okay?" he asked anxiously as he guided me to the chair.

"It's all in the delivery, dear," I heard my grandmother say with a chuckle although I couldn't see her. Gene was genuinely worried and I was equally confused. She'd only appeared when I was alone. Before now.

"I'm okay. I just felt faint for a second or two," I assured him. My cheeks were flushed, and I felt my pulse quicken.

"Cherry, he can't see or hear me." Her voice was calm and reassuring as she moved closer, stopping at the end of the table, clearly in my sight. My eyes shot back to Gene; a sense of urgency was exploding inside me.

"Remember when I told you that I'd heard my grandmother's voice? That I'd had an actual conversation with her?" I felt a lump in my throat, and my mouth was cottony. Gene waited, with curiosity painted all over his handsome face. When I looked up, Granny's smile widened. She was really enjoying this.

"Well", and I swallowed hard. "Now I can actually see her too," Gene quickly sat back in his chair and folded his arms across his chest. He'd listened and remained silent, but the look on his face was one you'd see on someone who'd just received some really bad news. I imagined he was thinking something along the lines of, *Oh crap, she's gone and lost her whole bag of marbles,* or that cracker-and-cheese expression my grandmother had loved so much; but I continued as his eyes bored into mine. "She actually told me about Saxby being kidnapped weeks ago. Well, she told me the details in a bunch of scary dreams."

He just sat and stared at me, scrutinizing my face. I felt a chill tingle down my spine and goose bumps rose up on my arms. *Even I wouldn't believe me*, I thought.

"Cherry, I really miss your grandmother too, but we both know where she is. We were there. We watched her body being lowered into the grave. She's always going to be in your heart, but you have to move on or this is going to make you crazy. You have to come to terms with the fact that she's in heaven with her husband and her family." He inhaled deeply, and I watched as he held his breath, probably trying to decide if there was anything more he could say, anything that he'd left out that could help his poor delusional wife cope. Anything that would reinforce the notion that I was just depressed about losing my grandmother at a time in my life when I may have felt I needed her the most.

"Cherise, be careful. Don't you go doing what I think you're about to do," my grandmother said, but I ignored her.

"No Gene, you're wrong. She's here, in this room, right now," I assured him. Gene looked at me for a long moment, and then he raised his eyebrows in disbelief. "She's standing not three feet away from you," I insisted. He wasn't going to argue with his mentally deranged wife, but I could tell by the expression on his face, and the tight crease in his forehead that he was all kinds of worried.

"Granny, please do something to show Gene that you're really here," and then they were both staring at me with confused expressions. My palms were wet, and I could feel the color draining from my face. I had to be paler than pale.

Finally she spoke up. "Okay." She mumbled. "Let me see what I can do," and her eyes scanned the room. I watched as she settled on the candle in the center of the table. "Oh Cherise, this is going to make my life messy, young lady," she warned before closing her eyes tightly. Her body moved toward the candle. After several grunts, her eyes popped open. "I just saw Charlotte do this yesterday," she commented, as she studied the candle. "It's easy-peasy when you first come, but a tad trickier once you're already here," she explained. "I'll need a moment to mull this over," she added. I looked back at Gene and he met my eyes with a humorous expression of sympathy. I felt like he was laughing on the inside, and suddenly I felt warm and clammy again.

"Granny, it's always worked before. What's wrong?" I asked, flustered and confused.

"So you're really not going to let this go, are you, Cherry?" a slightly challenge in his tone.

"No, I'm telling you the truth," and at precisely that moment, the candle lit itself. As the flame grew, I watched as Gene's eyes grew steadily wider.

Without looking at me he demanded, "Tell her to blow it out, then maybe I could believe this." He hesitated, and then watched my face to be sure I didn't blow toward the candle. I felt a brief twinge of guilt asking Granny to perform, like a trained circus animal, but Gene was leaving me no choice.

"Then you'll believe me? You'll believe I can see and speak to my grandmother? You promise?" I asked quickly.

"I promise," he assured me. I turned to my grandmother, who looked a little nervous. "Granny, please..." I asked politely. Like magic, the flame was extinguished. granny looked relieved, but Gene turned his chair to face the direction I'd been looking when I spoke to her. She and I had no time to relish the fact that she'd actually done it.

Holding me in his peripheral vision, he said, "Dottie, that was genuinely awesome. I'm so sorry..." We watched as his voice began to quiver while he focused on a spot several feet from where my grandmother actually stood. "...that I ever doubted my wife, but you gotta admit, this is all just a little bit creepy." and he looked back at me.

"Well that was just plain awkward," Granny said, her brown eyes filled with amusement. She was tickled with herself and I was greatly relieved. Now I could actually share all this madness with someone. And best of all, it was with my best friend.

Chapter Nineteen
Only A Dream

It was after 2 a.m. before Gene and I made it to bed. The dogs all had to go outside to potty and Michael called, saying he and Dustin had been driving the streets for hours with no luck. Evidently, Dustin and Jackson had gotten into a scuffle, big surprise; and had had some heated words before Jackson jumped out of the car, leaving them to search alone. I didn't even ask what it was about. The scuffle did explain Jackson's frazzled appearance when he'd arrived on our door step.

We found heather asleep in one of the spare rooms; she'd tunneled her way through the stacks of boxes to a twin bed and was out for the duration. Gene and I were astonished and perplexed at her ability to fall asleep with her son still missing. I still felt she knew more then she was admitting, but granny had assured me that Saxby was okay and that we needed to get some sleep before calling Jocelyn later in the morning. She'd explained that she needed to get back to Charlotte, whom she'd left happily haunting her family at her daughter's house. She said that Charlotte's great-grandson, Liam, had been the real reason she didn't want to cross over, and so spending time watching her daughter's family seemed to be softening her attitude.

"She enjoys spending time in Rockwell, pranking her kin people even more than she enjoys her bingo and beer in Vegas," Granny had announced with a chuckle.

Once in bed, in the dark room, before we fell asleep, Gene sprang straight up and blurted out, "She can see us having sex, can't she?"

I was lying on my side, my back to him, Ryan's long doxie nose in the crevice between my breasts. Gene's inquisitive concern smacked me like a wet washcloth and my eyes popped wide open. "No," I lied quickly. I rolled over, with the small dog's wet nose repositioned in my armpit. I couldn't see Gene's face but I felt around with my hand until I touched his body. "As long as there's a fan blowing, we're okay. Ghosts can't see through fast-moving air; come on, do you live under Plymouth Rock? That's like ghost 101, Gene," I insisted. "We're fine," I added nonchalantly. It was pitch-black but I could feel his eyes looking down at me, and although I couldn't see his expression, I could've guessed the look on his face. I felt his body slowly scoot down as he settled back in, and I held my breath as I turned back over. I so wanted to laugh. I did feel a tich guilty about deceiving him, now that he actually believed I could see and communicate with Granny, and I was using that new-found trust to my advantage. The thought of what he must've been thinking as he lay there trying to fall asleep, kept me smiling. Fortunately, we did have a fan in our room, strategically placed by the window to circulate the air but more than anything it acted as white noise, blocking the sound of cars passing by on the street directly outside our bedroom window. And to help minimize the effects of the Dachshunds passing gas too.

I'd begged Gene to switch rooms, we had three, but this was the master bedroom and the only one with a bathroom, hence, the noise-blocking fan. Several minutes later I felt myself drift off. Falling asleep was never a problem and I was exhausted, but lately, staying asleep was nearly impossible. I woke twice, both times with visions from the same dream. The really bad one my grandmother had stopped, but for some reason had suddenly started up again.

The second time, I awoke with a gasp as I caught myself from falling; tripping in that same dark place I'd been so many times before. The dream that took place in an old house; one of those creepy old mansions so old you'd only see them in black-and-white movies. It was always the same. It began with me outside the house, alone, staring up at a ten-foot beast of a wooden door. As I struggled to open the door, I would see a long, dark hallway with closed doors on both sides as far as I could see. I could hear muffled screams from several rooms, but was unable to tell if they were children or adults or both. The farther down the hall I walked, the clearer the screams became, then they'd become more desperate. I would reach what I thought must be the halfway point of the house, and a dark figure exploded out of nowhere, quickly approaching me from the opposite direction, head down and eyes glued to the floor. There was an almost oatmeal shade to his skin, and sand-colored hair and he would briskly attempt to pass me. And as he moved past me, there was an icy chill in the air. I would shiver, uncontrollably. Then I dropped to the floor. I'd thought I was there alone, but as I try to get to my feet, I saw Gene standing not three feet away from me, beads of sweat running off his forehead. A jolt of fear and a spike of adrenaline helped my legs stiffen so that I was able to stand. I inched my way forward, toward him. He was opening doors, searching the rooms for Sax, while I hobbled alongside him.

When we got to the very last door, I realized we had whittled down our number of possibilities, and Gene pointed to it and said, "He's got to be in there." I gripped the doorknob firmly with trembling hands, but hesitated for a moment. I could feel a cold draft coming from the crack under the door and I tried to force myself to remain calm. It didn't work. I inhaled deeply but it felt as though electrical pulses were coursing through me. My heart was pounding so hard it almost hurt. Was he in this room? And if he was, was he alive? I turned the doorknob and pushed with all my strength. Across the room, a boy about Saxby's age stood deathly still. He was tall and thin, maybe ninety pounds, with long black hair. He just stood, looking at me. I moved closer, until I could see his eyes. It was his eyes that startled me; they were the palest blue, maybe even gray, like the color of a pigeon. He stared straight through me, almost as if he was refusing to acknowledge that I was really there. Moments passed before I saw his bottom lip begin to quiver. His eyes filled with tears, yet his arms hung limply at his sides. Before I could say anything he threw himself down on an old dirty mattress, several inches from his feet, burying his face into a nasty-looking, yellow-stained pillow. His black hair almost covering it as he sobbed hysterically. I froze.

Twisting around, I looked at Gene, standing in the open doorway, and mouthed, "He's not here," and I watched as he slowly shook his head and I turned and made tracks for the door. Back in the hall, Gene pointed to a flight of stairs that neither of us had noticed, and we headed for it. The screams seemed louder and more desperate than before as we made our way up the steps. On the tenth set of steps my foot fell into a hole, a missing plank, but I caught myself and was able to regain my balance. I wanted to keep going, I wanted to find Saxby.

My eyes popped open and though consciously I knew that I'd just had that awful dream again, it didn't stop the feeling of having been threaded through the eye of a needle, again. What probably only lasted a few minutes, felt like a few years. As scary and vile as it was, I felt grateful that it was only a dream. My eyes flashed to the clock and I quickly eased myself out of the bed.

Granny's No Angel 119

Chapter Twenty
Saying It Out Loud

It was 6:30 a.m. when I checked the room Heather had been sleeping in and the bed was empty. She was gone. When I reached the top of the staircase, I could see her sitting at the kitchen table staring off into space as she sipped something from a coffee mug. When she saw me, she gave me a small tight smile without any happy in it.

As I fished the coffee and filters from the cabinet, I asked, "So you found the tea all right," not looking at her, and the box of tea sitting on the table in front of her. I wasn't really expecting an answer.

"Yeah, but I wish it was vodka," she said as she took a long sip from the cup.

"Yeah, you and me both," I admitted as I poured water into the coffee maker. Clearing her throat, she let out an animated sigh.

As she rattled her spoon against the mug, she blurted out, "You really, really hate Jackson, don't you?" I froze for a moment, completely flummoxed, before continuing to add sugar to my cup. I wanted to allow myself a moment to mull that question over before I answered. "Did you hear me?" she asked as I poured the coffee into my mug.

My back still to her, I answered, "Yes, I heard you," and I moved to the table, sitting down in the chair next to hers.

"You really hate him, don't you?" she pressed, visibly upset. She'd nailed my feelings for her husband on the head, but my instincts told me not to kick someone when they're already down; now wasn't the best time to talk smack about Jackson. Her hair hid her eyes, but I could see fresh tear tracks down both sides of her cheeks. As I looked into her face, I waited, because she acted as if she was going to add something, but then decided against it. Her eyes now planted firmly on her cup, I decided to level with her. I kept my gaze on her, hoping that she wouldn't look up until I'd finished what I had to say.

"I think as highly of him as he does of me," I offered honestly. She looked as though she was wrestling with my words for a few moments before taking another long sip from her mug. "It's like this, Heather," I continued, before giving her time to say anything. "Sometimes I just want to scream at you and ask who you are and what did you do with my sister?" and I threw one hand under my butt cheek...maybe for added strength, I'm not really sure.

"Once upon a time you were easy going and kicked back. You were funny and you were kind. Now, you're just all judgmental and mean. And when I say mean...I mean...black-hearted; stabbing people in the back, not-giving-two-shits mean. You talk shit about everyone and it just makes you look so ugly. I know we're blood, but I don't consider you anything close to a friend anymore, and we used to be so, so very close. Here lately, my dogs treat me better than you do. That's what I think Jackson has done to you. But I also believe you've allowed him to. So, to answer your question...yeah, I pretty much *don't* like Jackson."

My eyes dropped to the cup in my hand. *Did I say too much? Did I say it right?* I was doubting myself. The last thing I wanted to do while her son was missing was to upset her. She was my sister. Part of me hoped that what I'd said would be the *oomph* she needed to realize that she'd been settling; settling for less than she deserved. Without looking up at her, I began blowing nervously at my coffee. It wasn't hot in the room, but the situation was and I could feel the heat rising in my cheeks. Heather was my older sister and I'd never said anything before, not anything like I'd just said to her. Although I'd always felt that Jackson courted controversy, rather than my sister, from the beginning of their relationship; I'd never ever spoken of it until now. When I was finally brave enough to look up, another trickle of tears had dribbled down her cheeks. Suddenly, our eyes met and we sat in silence. Gene was at the top of the stairs, and one of the dogs must've shimmed under his feet because first there was a yelp, followed by his fist colliding with the wall. The loud bang caused us both jump and turn around towards the stairs. "If you're trying for stealth, you're failing horribly," I said, with both humor and concern. Gene ignored my comment and headed for the back door. I watched as the dogs thundered across the room and out the open door. Even little Tomorrow was running with all she had. When I looked back at my sister, she was chewing on her bottom lip, deep in thought, her eyes lowered.

When she finally looked up, she asked, "So, have you told Gene about our discussion last night in the bathroom yet?"

He was leaning against the door frame between the kitchen and living room, arms crossed, looking almost alienated from what he'd usually consider hot gossip. I looked at him for a brief moment before going eye-to-eye with my sister.

"You asked me not to and so I didn't," I scoffed, annoyed. "But now, since you've brought it up, maybe you should tell him," I added.

"Yeah, you should tell me," Gene said with a teasing tone. He was a picture; wrinkled t-shirt, sweatpants, and wild, tangled hair.

"Dustin's my father," she blurted out. Tears streamed down her face, as if this was the first time she'd actually accepted that fact and quickly wiped her face with the back of her hand. When I looked up for Gene's reaction, his eyes were big, but not a word left his mouth.

My fingers were drumming the table nervously when Gene blurted out, "Well, your sister sees dead people," and somehow managed to keep a serious expression on his face.

Heather glanced my way and I froze. "Yeah, and leprechauns fly out of my butt," she said with a crack of laughter.

Within seconds, she'd gone from weeping to laughter, and I just smiled up at Gene. Not in the usual way. No, Gene hated it when I gave him that smile. I rolled my eyes and shook my head from side to side, making sure it was known that I was purposely keeping my pie-hole shut. That I was only tolerating the situation, rather than going full-on crazy bitch at him.

Heather was clueless, which might be the real reason my husband's still alive today. She must have thought Gene was just throwing that glob of silliness out there to make her situation seem better. Several awkward, silent moments passed before her cell phone rang. She pulled it from her sweater pocket and put it to her ear. After a couple of eye rolls, yeahs, okays, and sures, accompanied by several shrugs, she ended the call and shoved the phone back into her pocket. *It must've been either Jackson or my mother*, I thought.

Chapter Twenty-One
Taking The First Step

After a quick breakfast, and when I say breakfast, I really mean a hint of breakfast: toast and jelly, Gene tidied up the kitchen while Heather and I showered and got dressed. We were going to meet Jocelyn at ten o'clock at her office across town. The phone call Heather had received was from my mother, informing her that Jackson never showed up after leaving our house, and that she'd decided to take the kids to the park to take their minds off the many questions they were asking. Bottom line: She was actually making herself useful. She'd told Heather she wanted to help, but we both knew that when our mother said *help*, she really meant that she wanted to be *all up in your business*. With the list Jackson had dropped, the one with two names already crossed off, we headed for Jocelyn's place of business. During the drive, my sister stared out the window, all zombie-like, while I tried to focus on the traffic, anything that'd keep my thoughts off my nephew. Was he scared? Was he warm and fed? I soon realized it was a battle I couldn't win.

"What if he's....you know," Heather said quietly. She was about to say a word I knew if I said out loud, would gum up in my throat like wet bread and probably choke me.

"Shut up," the words flew from my lips before I could stop them. Her face was pained, and I realized my fingers were gripping the steering wheel so tightly my knuckles were white. "He's going to be fine" I said, with my eyes on the traffic. "Don't even think that he's not, okay?" and I inhaled slowly, trying to calm myself as I let my breath out. "Okay," she repeated in just above a whisper.

I knew he was going to be okay. Granny had assured me he was going to be okay. Then why was I so worried about him not being okay? I pressed the accelerator to the floorboard, suddenly feeling as if we needed to step things up in our search for Saxby. I was beginning to lose faith that everything was going to be fine; faith I'd thought I had.

Once there, Heather answered the many questions Jocelyn had for her, including how she knew the people on Jackson's handwritten list. Chelly and Keene were the names that had been scratched out, although my sister said she had no idea about anyone's last name. I tried my best to stay out of the way and

Granny's No Angel 127

allow Jocelyn to do her job and investigate, but it seemed as if it was taking way more time than we had. Remembering the horrible dream I'd relived last night, the clock seemed to be ticking way too slowly, and I felt a sudden urge to scream.

I left Heather and Jocelyn in the office, and I walked to the picture window in the front room. Immediately my eyebrows shot down in confusion. I could feel the hair pulling at my temples, and it wasn't because my ponytail was too tight. I saw Jackson, maybe three cars down, strategically parked on the street, in such a way that he'd see us leaving. Now he could see me looking out the window and stood in front of his car staring intently at me, as if he was warning or threatening me. The sign in front of Jocelyn's office read, Cones' Criminal and Civil Investigations, and it was clear that Jackson was not happy that we were there. He had told us to stay out of it. That he had it handled. But did he? I drew in a deep breath, trying to remind myself that the man standing out there was Heather's husband, the father of her four children; a guy who'd just made some awful choices. Choices my grandmother had assured me she was required to fix before she could progress to her desired destination. *It will all turn out all right for him* she'd said. He looked calmer as he stared back at me and I almost relaxed enough to smile back; but his smile was chilling and that stopped me. He was cold and distant. Before I'd put that together, I felt Heather's stare as she stood beside me.

"What the..?" she said following my gaze, and then turned and headed for the front door.

"Don't," I demanded in disbelief, as she flew through the open door and out into the parking lot. As I stood staring, Jocelyn appeared from behind me and put a reassuring hand on my shoulder. We watched as Jackson and Heather hugged each other, as you'd expect two terrified parents would do.

"Do you think you can help us find him?" I asked as we continued to look out the window.

"Yeah, but I think your sister and brother-in-law need to be honest with me. I believe that no one snatches a child unless someone has taken things to an extremely dangerous level," she said. "And not going to the police with this might end up being the biggest mistake of their lives. I have resources, but the police have more," she added.

I stepped back and veered to my left until I felt a chair against my calves and plopped down. "About that," and I cringed as I undid my ponytail and shook my head, freeing my hair from the confines of the hair tie I was sure was adding to my newly-developing headache. "Did my sister happen to mention anything about there being a huge possibility her husband might have stolen some drugs from a dealer?" I watched as she shrugged; confusion on her face.

"No, she didn't mention that or that she had any idea why her son was taken," she said, her expression hardening. "But you know I can't help you, Cherry, if you aren't honest with me. You understand that, right? You need to tell me everything you know about all of this, like where the drugs are, when the husband took them? Only then can I decide where to start. I can't help you find your nephew if you don't first help me understand what's really going on," she said. I couldn't argue with that.

She went to her office to retrieve a notepad she'd used while questioning my sister. I noticed not much was written on it. I plunged ahead and told her everything I knew, which was everything Heather also knew but had chosen to not share with her.

I didn't tell her about Granny. I decided that that wouldn't really help anything, but I did tell her about the dreams I'd been having. She listened, but she seemed not to give them any value within her investigation. I'm not entirely sure, but I think she was sizing up my grip on reality. I do know that when we left her office, I didn't feel any better about the situation than I had before we'd arrived. At that point I was just obsessed with an unexplainable need to talk to my grandmother. I dropped Heather off at her house and made a bee-line for home.

Chapter Twenty-Two
Out With The Old, And The New Is Good

It was three long days after our meeting with Jocelyn before the whole Jackson fiasco finally came to an end and Saxby was reunited with his parents. It ended without incident or any police involvement. Apparently my sister-in-law is really good at what she does. Granny showed up the same evening, the day Heather and I went to Jocelyn's office. She gave me an address in an old abandoned neighborhood that frankly, being a native of Santa Barbara, was an area that I was surprised to find I didn't even know existed. She was adamant that I pass the address on to Jocelyn, rather than get involved. I promised I would if she'd do me the favor of sharing the dream I'd been having with Jocelyn, even if just once, so that she could see the things I'd seen, hoping that even one of those scary things might be of help to her. Also, she might at least have reason to doubt her clearly obvious, newly-formed opinions of me being a total whack job.

Granny agreed, and I did as she asked, and stayed completely out of it although it wasn't easy. Jocelyn took the drugs, or skunk weed as she called it, that had been hidden and stored in my Granny's basement and arranged to make a trade with the man Jackson had been selling the marijuana for. I found out later that the guy's name is Philip Hole, or at least that's the name that he gave my sister-in-law. Seriously, Philip Hole? That does not sound like a big-time, scary drug dealer to me, not that I've ever known any. Jocelyn spoke to Heather and Jackson after she brought my nephew home, making it very clear that if she ever caught wind of any more illegal shenanigans from either of them, she'd go straight to the authorities and have their children removed from their home. She'd put her whole career on the line to help Gene and me with this shady predicament, and she wanted them to know it. I believe my sister understood.

Heather took the whole experience very seriously and left Jackson two days after Saxby's return. Gene and I agreed to rent my grandmother's house to her and the kids, and she enrolled them into a highly-regarded charter school close by. She also found a part-time position within the local art community, hoping that after everyone settled into a new routine, she'd be able to go back to her painting, which she loves and was really missing. The best part of all that was happening, apart from Sax's safe return, was that Heather and I began spending some fun time together, and I have to say that it feels wonderful having my sister back. She admitted to me that many red flags had been raised, and that things had been going south with her and Jackson's relationship for some time, but that she didn't feel she had any real options or resources. She felt forced to stay and make the best of it. We're both more relaxed now that some of the bumpier bumps have been smoothed out. We've had some wonderful walks on the beach, with and without dogs and kids, gone to some colorful art shows and festivals, and even done some adventuring on short day trips. When we get together, it's like we're kids again, joking around, laughing, having fun and just enjoying everything more than ever. Something I've been wanting for a very long time.

Gene and I discussed it and agreed that we wanted to pay his sister her usual fee for her services, and we made the trip across town to do just that. At first she gave us some grief and flat-out objected, "Family doesn't charge family," she insisted, acting as if our offer was out of the question. In her crisp, runway-sheik pantsuit accompanied by the click of her high heels pacing the tile floor, she walked in circles around the room.

Granny's No Angel 134

"My grandmother once told me that love and loyalty can be both a blessing and a curse, but you should always reward someone for going above and beyond when you are able. Gene and I are able," I confided. "You are responsible for the most positive outcome we could have imagined Jocelyn, and for that I am forever grateful."

"And don't forget about the dreams," Gene said, interrupting me. I watched Jocelyn's face as she blinked in surprise at the mention of the dreams. It was clear that Granny had given her at least a taste of what I had been seeing. And my dreams had already begun to reflect the happier things in my life. It was nice.

Although I've always been curious, I never did ask about the little boy in the room. Jocelyn said that I would not want to know what had happened in that house. She was right, so I zipped it and never brought the subject up again. Finally, she agreed to accept our check and we were all happy to put the whole Jackson experience behind us.

I'd visited with my grandmother a total of eight times in the month of September, Charlotte tagging along with her at least half the time. Gene had taken the whole thing with a sarcastic grain of salt, and began asking numerous times during the day if the ladies were *in the house.* And always with a smirk of amusement if I confirmed that they were there. Although I'd explained exactly what Granny had told me about Charlotte and her situation, he was still having a hard time even grasping her existence. Granny reminded me that for some people it was that way with almost anything; unless you were able to lay your own two eyes on something, it just remained a mystery. *Almost like a fairy tale* she'd said. That held true for Gene. He'd accepted that Granny was there, but openly teased me about Charlotte really being there or even being real. When Charlotte did accompany my grandmother and Gene was in the room, a mischievous grin appeared on her face as she examined him with fascination and plotted. She was thoroughly enjoying the whole *haunting* aspect that her present place in transition allowed her.

"She takes her family in Rockwell on a real carnival ride," Granny told me with a snicker. When Granny objected to what she must have known Miss Charlotte was thinking and chastised her for even considering pranking Gene, Charlotte would give her a pout, before starting her minor tantrum. "If looks could kill, I'd be six feet under right now," my grandmother giggled.

"Dottie, you're not my boss and when I figure out how to pull it off, you're going straight to hell with a pocket full of squirt guns, do you hear me?" she scoffed. She then followed her threat with a little grin. "Oh crap, did I say that out loud?" she chuckled, her eyes twinkling. I was never absolutely certain, but it was an awfully huge coincidence that whenever Charlotte was around, Gene would slam his palm against his forehead; a lot, and it wasn't something he'd usually do.

My grandmother would say, "Charlotte, behave!" in a harsh tone after he'd smack himself, so maybe it was the Napkin Nazi doing something to him after all. I guess I'll never really know. She had begun to grow on me. The fact that she enjoyed our dogs was a pleasant plus, and more than I could say for some of the " living" people in our life. She often referred to them as the little pipsqueaks or monkeys, and she did so endearingly. If the pups were outside and came into the house to find Granny and Char visiting, they'd run around in circles like little firecrackers, bucking and barking, excited to see our colorful non-physical visitors. In time, Gene didn't have to ask if the ladies were *in the house* if Tomorrow was close by, because she'd let him know in her own way. Intuitively, the little dog knew she could trust them, even though she usually shied away from strangers. She'd inch her way forward, nose high in the air, sniffing with each tiny step. You could almost see her rubber-lipped grin as she trotted circles around her guests. Jennifer, however, was quite the opposite. She'd slink off under a table, head down, and tail between her legs; curious, but watching from a safe distance. Angelina, Princess and Pretzel didn't much care if our visitors were there or not, they felt indifferent about the whole thing. Brad and Ryan were the funniest of them all. They'd both look directly at Granny, balancing on their bottoms, front paws dangling in the begging position, waiting for her to hook them up as she'd done so many times before. She'd feel guilty and talk me into getting them a treat from the fridge. Of course I would, and she often used that moment to say her goodbyes, maybe as a distraction so I wouldn't feel upset about her leaving. It worked for a while, but as time went on, I knew she was preparing me for the inevitable. I could feel it deep down in my heart.

Granny's No Angel 138

Chapter Twenty-Three
Transformations

June 2013

The months came and went, and before I realized it, we were approaching the one-year anniversary of my grandmother's passing. Of course the date didn't affect me the same way it did other family members because I saw Granny on a regular, well, actually on more of a sporadic basis. The last time I'd seen her she'd mentioned in her special roundabout way, two things that were weighing heavily on my mind, matters I'm sure she'd given much thought to.

"People are who they are dear and if you can accept and appreciate the role they play in your life, there's more peace in that." I looked at her curiously at first, but within moments I knew whom she was referring to. It had been months since I'd seen my mother, although we'd spoken on the phone a time or two. Neither Heather, Michael, nor Gene or I had ever disclosed to her, Harry, or Dustin the fact that we knew all three of us Legg children were fathered by Mr. Dustin Jase Paul, Granny's best friend's son.

Michael was still torqued off about it, and hadn't seen or spoken to my mother or Harry since moving in with Dustin, although Gene and I had taken his kids over to visit her a few times. He told me he felt as though his relationship with our father, Harry, had been based on a huge lie, and he was sure Harry had to have known about our mother's other relationship. He took Dustin's side, plain and simple, and claimed that he and Dustin were victims of my mother's villainous behavior. Even though my brother and mother's relationship had totally deteriorated, Gene and I watched as something remarkably positive developed because of it.

Michael began to really enjoy his single parent status. He was no longer just a weekend dad. With Dustin's help and support, my brother's children went from spending weekends with him to spending a solid two weeks a month in his house. My brother gave up loose women and bars for coaching T-ball and attending swimming lessons. Fatherhood was finally fitting him like a seasoned player's batting glove, and it was refreshing as his little sister, to witness that transformation. Gene was also impressed. He called Mike a crackerjack of a dad, and said he'd never have believed such a change was possible if he hadn't witnessed it himself. That made two of us.

After talking with Gene about all the mixed feelings I was harboring toward my mother, he encouraged me to make a special trip over to her house, alone, and visit with her. I agreed, but oddly enough, I knew deep down I was doing it more for Granny's sake than mine or even my mother's. And then, before I'd decided a hundred percent that I was actually going to go through with the visit, a quote that I'd always adored and hadn't given any thought to in years, popped into my head at just the right moment, and sealed the deal for me. Mark Twain had said: *When in doubt, do right. This will gratify some people and astonish the rest.* I'm sure I was more astonished than anyone else about dropping by, out of the blue, to see my mother, knowing what I did. It wasn't on my top-ten-favorite-things-to-do list, but I was sure it would give Granny and my mother some gratification. So I did cruise over to my mom's house, deciding at the last minute not to call first, and on my way there, a song I dearly loved came on the radio, lifting my spirits and saddening me at the same time. "All My Life," was Spank's and my song. As he was riding shotgun with me, I'd sing this song to him, my beloved Dachshund, sometimes at the top of

my lungs. He'd just sit and look back at me adoringly, as if he

understood every word.

"All My Life"
By Aaron Neville and Linda Ronstadt

Am I really here in your arms
This is just like I dreamed it would be.
I feel like we're frozen in time
And you're the only one I can see.

Hey, I've looked all my life for you
Now you're here.
Hey, I've spent all my life with you
All my life.

And I never really knew how to love.
I just hope somehow I'll see.
Oh I ask for a little help from above.
Send an angel down to me.

Hey, I've looked all my life for you
Now you're here.
Hey, I've spent all my life with you
All my life.

I never thought that I could feel a love so tender.
Never thought I could let those feelings show,
But now my heart is on my sleeve
And this love will never leave,
I know,
I know

Hey, I've looked all my life for you
And now you're here, now you're here
Hey, I've spent all my life with you
All my life, all my life.

Hey, I've looked all my life for you
And now you're here, now you're here
Hey, I've spent all my life with you
All my life.

I really missed my little man. Sometimes, he'd been the only real light in my life before Gene came along. I felt a large lump in my throat as I stared out the windshield, parked outside my mother's house. Knuckles rapped on the window, on the passenger's side, just as a horn blasted from a passing car beside me, startling me out of my daydream. I pushed the van door open, slamming it shut as I edged my way around to the curb where Peggy stood. She was studying my face. "What's wrong?" she asked. "You look like you just lost your best friend," she added.

"Nothing," I said. "Nothing at all," I added in a mumble. She gestured for me to come to her and then stretched her arms out wide.

"Come here," she said in her best motherly tone. I did, and she swallowed my body in a protective mamma-bear hug, her white fluffy sweater soft and fragrant, like her. We went into the house and she offered me some tea. I went to the fridge and rooted around, finding an open bottle of Chardonnay. I set it on the counter and opened the cabinet looking for a glass.

She stood watching me, balling her hands nervously in front of her. "I'm actually so happy you decided to stop by," she said as I poured the wine. When I turned to respond, tears were streaming down her cheeks. "Oh Cherise," she said. I leaned back against the counter and watched as she sat down at the kitchen table. "I've really been thinking a lot about my mother, lately missing her, you know," and it was as if her words were reaching deep down inside me and squeezing my insides. Instantly I felt this huge ball of guilt lodge itself in my gut, although I wasn't entirely sure why. "Please, won't you sit with me?" and with a quick nod, I sat in the chair across from her. I sipped slowly from the glass as I watched her fidget like a nervous child, obviously trying to muster up a way to say what it was she felt compelled to tell me. I studied her face, and I felt at an uncomfortable disadvantage about where this conversation might be going. I'm sure she knew that.

Not three heartbeats later, she drew her breath in sharply, and with widened eyes she asked, "Did you feel that?" My gaze moved from her and settled on the object slowly materializing behind her. A sense of relief washed over me when I realized that it was Granny. I offered my hand to my mother, maybe unconsciously as a distraction, but she latched onto it, smiling and sniveling, and with fresh tears streaming down her cheeks she said,

"I think my mom has been here, visiting me, but I don't know that for certain, because I can't see her. Sometimes, it's as if I can feel her presence, and Cherise," with her free hand wiping the tears from her cheek, "I really want to speak to her just one last time," she said softly. I was on the verge of tears myself. *How long has it been since all three of us have been in the same room together?* I thought to myself.

"It's been a long while," my grandmother answered, with sadness in her eyes.

"Maybe if you just sat and spoke to her," I offered, with a quick glance at Granny and was relieved when the kitchen phone rang. Mom let go of my hand and excused herself. She migrated to the living room with the phone to her ear.

"It's Harry," my grandmother announced proudly. *She's getting this ghosty thing down to a science,* I thought. "And she really needs an order of fries to go along with that shake," she snickered before turning her attention back to me. With a brackish taste in my mouth from my own tears, I got up to refill my glass. I was breathing a little easier knowing my mother wanted to talk about Granny and nothing else.

"Why does she think you've been here?" I asked, fixing my gaze on the bottle.

"Well, I wanted to comfort her, maybe make her feel a tad bit better; you should really hear what rolls around in that gal's head" and she shook her head back and forth slowly, her smile gone. "I tried to do something with my limited powers to help make her feel better about the way we left things, but after a while I realized it was just more difficult than I'd first thought. Now I realize I'm going to need your help dear, if you don't mind," and my forehead scrunched together as I looked her in the eye.

"I'm seriously confused," I admitted.

"Well, Cherry, I'm going to ask you to fib; just a little white lie," and instinctively, she glanced through the open door way to ensure that my mother wasn't headed our way. "I want you to tell her that you and I had a conversation the day before I passed, one that you'd never shared with her. Maybe say that you felt, at the time, it was just something better left unsaid, but now you've had a change of heart." I sat down, placing the bottle on the table, my eyes glued to her face. "Time is a funny thing dear.

Granny's No Angel 146

It sneaks up on you like a windshield wiper on a bug. Peggy believes that she let me down in my golden years. She's beating herself up over the fact that as my oldest child, she didn't properly care for me as she thinks she should have. I want you to convince her that she did just fine."

"But we both know she didn't," I whispered, trying to avoid Mom hearing me.

"Yes Cherry, it seems that way, but she had her reasons and the path she was walking wasn't the easiest one."

" I've never minded getting old, dear, and I'm so grateful I didn't end up being a terrible burden on anyone. Well, except you and Gene of course." I wanted to tell her she was never, ever a burden; I even scooted my butt to the edge of my seat, but she held up a finger for me to let her finish. I did.

"I had a wonderful life. I had the privilege of living in my own home and pretty much on my terms. I didn't stay too long, in fact, if I had it to do over again, I'm sure I wouldn't change a thing," and a little smile touched the corners of her mouth, "Well maybe I would have eaten more pie" and she smiled as broadly as she could. "Could you do that for me, Cherise?" she asked.

Granny's No Angel 147

I pulled in a deep breath and noticed Peggy was on her way back with the phone in her hand.

"That was your dad," she said, before realizing what she'd said. "Well, it was Harry," she corrected herself, in a nervous-sounding whisper.

"He's still my dad," I muttered. Looking into my face with a blank stare, she sat down, crossing her arms tightly around her stomach.

"Where were we?" She asked. My grandmother stepped up behind her, silently shadowing her to remind me why she was there and what she wanted me to do. I grabbed the bottle in front of me and poured its contents into my glass. It suddenly felt heavy.

Taking a deep breath, I said, "I really need to share something with you," and as the last word left my mouth, I watched Granny's image fade until it disappeared completely. My mother's forehead creased in curiosity, and then she seemed to be preparing herself for the worst. My mood shifted automatically, as if someone else was driving. My face felt relaxed and a smile formed smoothly on my lips. Then I heard myself say, "You're gonna like this Mom."

Chapter Twenty-Four
The Sun Will Come Out Tomorrow

August 16, 2013

My journey is ending," Granny said.

"And you're never coming back?" It wasn't a question really. She'd tried to prepare me for this moment since that first evening we'd spoken at my kitchen table.

"You're going to be just fine, Cherise," she assured me. "You and Gene need to be thinking about that Hawaiian vacation you haven't taken yet," she added. That was the second thing she'd said that had been weighing heavily on my mind. I believe now that I pushed the thought of going away as far down as I possibly could, afraid that once we actually left for Hawaii, my grandmother's visits would end. My thinking was, if I stayed close to home maybe she wouldn't leave.

Several days ago Granny and Miss Char had arrived early in the evening with a rather strange request. "Cherise, I'd like you to purchase a card for a great-grandson and have it in the mail for me tomorrow. I have an address and Charlotte's going to tell you what to write inside."

"Okay," I said and grabbed a pen and notepad from my desk drawer. "And who is this for?" I asked, anxious to know more.

"Does it really matter, dear?" Charlotte asked curtly.

"Well you're asking me to do something for you," I reminded her. It was clear that she wasn't particularly concerned about the impression she made; just that this task be done.

"It's for her great grandson Liam," Granny answered. It was quiet for a brief minute, and then Charlotte, looking down at the floor, muttered just loud enough for me to hear her.

"I'm sorry, Cherise. I appreciate your help, I really do. I just miss my family and I hate the situation I'm in," and she turned, almost like a child looking for an approving look from Granny.

"She's just upset that she has to ask, dear. She likes to do things for herself," my grandmother explained. I sat down and with pen in hand, looked up at Charlotte.

She straightened her shoulders and her expression softened.

"*Dear Liam*", she began. Before I could start writing, my eyes met my grandmother's and she signaled me with a thumbs up. *"Even though we've never actually met, I want you to know that I was there with you the day you were born. I want you to know that I love you and your brother and sister with all my heart and I will always be there, watching over and protecting all of you the best that I am able. I will try my damnedest to be there when you turn twenty-one and crack your first beer, and play your first slot machine. I will always be your guardian angel."*

Several silent moments passed, so I looked up as she turned back to Granny for another nod of approval, and then back to me. "Should I add my name?" she asked. Her question actually brought me back to the reality of the moment, and I was unsure of what to tell her. My grandmother stepped up and with an arm cradled over her shoulder, she whispered something into Charlotte's ear. The two women looked at each other and then Char looked back at me. "Thank you so much for doing this for me," and I could feel the warmth of gratitude coming from her as if it were a tight hug.

"You're very welcome," I told her. With that she turned, and in only two small steps... disappeared into thin air.

My grandmother explained that she'd finally convinced her new-found friend that it was time to go.

"Her name is Charlotte Louise Turner, and she is the mother of three children, all girls," she said. "Charlotte, Debby, and Terry," she added, pleased with herself for remembering. She gave me the address and before I had time to ask her how this was ever going to work, she smiled at me with pure amusement on her face. "I'm going to pull some strings and have the postmark changed and schedule the card's arrival for just the right time," she explained.

Very clever, I thought to myself.

"Yes it is, dear, and everyone wins," she said, still amused and satisfied with herself. I tucked the information into a pocket of my purse, and bought and mailed the card the next day. And now, Charlotte was on track, and Saxby was safe, so I knew that my grandmother was finally pickle bound.

The night before she left, I'd found Gene sitting on the sofa, humming the tune "The Sun Will Come Out Tomorrow," an appropriate song as any for a rescue dog. He was cuddling the little Chihuahua to his chest. Six small Dachshunds lie sprinkled about our living room floor, all sleeping soundly. I sat next to him and he took my hand and gave it a squeeze.

"What's bothering you?" He asked. I looked into his eyes with a question that I'd wrestled with since Charlotte's departure.

"If you could come back after you die, would you?" I asked. I guess I expected a look of puzzlement, or even a little surprise at the nature of my question, since he did know about my grandmother and Charlotte, but he didn't go to either of those places. He paused for a long moment, ceased the soft ear rubbing, and looked me straight in the eye.

"I want to do whatever you want to do," and his face was full of sincerity and love. Just as I laid my head on his shoulder, I felt a swish, as soft as a feather against my face. She was there, I just knew it. My bottom lip began trembling slightly as I realized she was really leaving. The one woman I'd admired the most. The woman that made me feel the most loved was never going to be there again. I was going to miss the way her eyes widened with a childish twinkle when she was tickled, and how she always had the right answers for me. August 16th, a Friday night, was the last time I spoke with Granny. She was only there for a few minutes, telling

Granny's No Angel 153

me she had a window of time within which she had to transition. After our goodbyes, she left, and I cried until there were no more tears, had some wine, and then dragged myself to bed. Just as I settled in, I felt Gene's hand touch the center of my back. I wasn't in any mood to be comforted, or touched for that matter. I just wanted to go to sleep and mourn my loss for the second time, quietly, in my wine stupor.

"Are you awake?" he whispered.

"Yes," I answered reluctantly.

"Well remind me to tell you about something I found today," he said in a groggy voice.

"Okay" and I pulled the sheet up to my nose, wiping the moisture from my face. Minutes ticked by and my mind wouldn't let go of what he'd just said. Maybe it was a good thing really; it was distracting my misplaced feelings of abandonment, at least temporarily. I turned back over and eased closer to him. "What did you find?" I asked with a parched voice.

He smacked his lips and made several obnoxious sounds with his mouth before answering me. "I was getting ready to delete all the files that I took from your mother's computer and guess what I found?" I lifted myself up on my elbow, checking to see if he was really awake or just talking in his sleep. He was awake and so were most of the dogs.

"What did you find, Gene?" I asked.

"Well, it seems your mother has been keeping a diary too," he said rubbing his nose.

"Really…" I said with my interest piqued.

"Yeah…and the best part is that she scanned a notebook or many notebooks, because the dates go back more than forty years."

I lay back down, Jennifer at my chest looking for a warm place to snooze. "Well just delete it tomorrow," I said as I turned my pillow, looking for a cool spot.

No problemo," he whispered.

"Good," I said finally after several minutes of thought. "We don't need to open *that* can of worms."

The End.

Or is it?

Made in the USA
Middletown, DE
10 May 2018